When the Past Comes Knock'N

ISBN 978-0-615-55722-9

From my Heart to Yours

First I would like to thank GOD, all things are possible through him. I want to thank my parents for always encouraging me to follow my dreams and always being the extra push I needed to get things done. I owe much thanks to my sister for always encouraging me to follow my dreams, she initially encouraged me to publish my book. To all of my friends and family members I extend many thanks, for all of their encouraging words and support. I dedicate "When the Past Comes Knock'N" to my family, without their support I wouldn't have had the courage to take such a leap. Thank you all!

Always follow your dreams and know that anything is possible when you put your mind and heart into it. Don't let anyone tell you what you can't do.

Chapter One

Every bone in my body filled with rage as another man's voice echoed through the other end of the phone. I double checked to make sure the phone number that I dialed was correct and sure enough it was.

I couldn't do anything but laugh," Can you believe this shit dog?"

Shawn chuckled, "I don't even know why you're sweating her."

We both sat back and enjoyed a laugh, as smoke filled the air. I knew my girl did her dirt once upon a time but I thought we both had put our playa cards away. I damn sure dogged a couple of women when I was younger but since I had been kicking it with her those days were a thing of the past. I questioned my reasons for even kicking it with her, lately she had been giving me all kinds of doubts. It was bad enough she was a stripper, I had enough money to support her but she insisted on being Ms. Independent and wouldn't let me take care of her bills. She accepted money from me, which I figured she used to buy shoes, or clothes but nonetheless, she still wouldn't leave the pole alone. I knew she had, had a lot of sex partners, so did I but all that was supposed to be behind us. I couldn't hold her up for her track record, especially if mine was probably just as long, if not longer. I wasn't sure what it was but I knew something was going on with her. I could only imagine what a woman especially one such as herself would say if another woman answered my phone, I wouldn't hear the end of it. It is one thing to piss off a woman but another thing to piss off a Black Woman. I always picked my battles wisely with women, even when you're right, you're wrong. I knew better than to just attack her about who the man was, instead I just waited for her to call and give me an excuse about who he was, or why the nigga picked up her phone.

My phone buzzed on the couch as her name popped up on the screen, "Wad up?"

Her voice was so sweet and innocent, "Hey baby, sorry about that. I'm at my brother's house and I asked him to answer the phone when I was in the bathroom."

I knew she was talking some sideways bullshit but I let it slide because I didn't give a damn any more. Two of her brothers were always in and out of prison, one was in college, and the other was always working so it was very unlikely that she was with either of them. I didn't even want to think about where she could have been, or who she was with so I dismissed the situation and kept the conversation moving. It was always one thing or another with her; she never could tell me the whole story or the truth about anything.

Looking at Shawn," It's alright Trina. Are you coming by later?"

She hesitated then cleared her throat," Umm yea…..I'll be by when I get off work."

I bullshitted with her for a minute then we hung up. Trina wasn't the type of chick that you married or even brought home to mama. She was a good listener and an easy fuck but other than that she didn't have much to offer. For some reason or another I was semi-close to her. I wouldn't say I loved her but she was the only person I found myself sleeping with and that was rare. I usually stuck to the bottom bitch theory of having three or four girls, but with her, she was my one and only. I met her one night at a club; I guess it's true what they say about meeting women at the club, they are good for a few nights but they usually aren't the females you settle down in a relationship with. I spotted her posted at the bar with her girls, they were all good looking but there was something about her that had me going wild. Every guy in the building was trying to get her attention but she picked me out of the crowd. I brought her friends some drinks then took her by the hand and we settled at a table in the back

of the club. We talked for a while, danced to a few songs, and she tossed

me her number. My intention was to pull a one night stand but night after

night we ended up in my bed and eventually we stopped just having sex

and started dating each other exclusively, or so I thought. I won't deny

that we had a good time together but trying to build a future with her is

like waiting for a boat at the airport, the shit just wasn't going to happen.

Shawn shook his head," So what shit was she talking about this

time?"

I laughed," Nigga, you know her, same old shit. She probably was

fucking some nigga, talking about she was at her brother's house."

I knew what Shawn was thinking but he didn't say anything. Most

of my friends didn't have anything good to say about her because she had

tricked most of the nigga's in the city off. She was one of the reasons why

strippers had a bad rep. I normally could read women like a June edition

of Sports Illustrated but she played a good game. Unpredictable women

are sexy but there is a difference between being sneaky and being

unpredictable. We finished playing madden and blew a few l's before I had

to hit the studio.

Grabbing my phone," Iight bro I'll get at you."

Shawn was my right hand man he kicked it to me real and didn't hesitate to call me out on my shit. He kept it real about me still fucking with Trina but he said his piece and let the situation rest. He wasn't one of those people that went on and on about the same thing once he said what he had to say that was the end of the discussion. Shawn saw right through her bullshit from day one, while my dumbass still fed into it. He was probably one of my only friends who hadn't tried to bend her ass over backwards and make her touch her toes. Shawn and I grew up together he was like a brother to me, we went to the same schools from K to 12th grade. I didn't trust too many cats but I trusted Shawn with my life. I drove down 7mile doing about 50 mph banging Icewood, thinking about my life and how far I had come.

When I pulled up to the studio it was a little past seven o'clock, Trigger and Mack were already posted in the booth making magic. I could hear the music from the studio flowing into the streets. I loved the sound of real Rap instead of that little bubble gum rap that the radio played. I felt like it was my duty to change the music game because artist in the music industry now only talked about wrist watches and hoes, music was going in a downward spiral.

I walked through the studio doors, "Wad up doe?"

They both gave me daps," Wad up boy!"

I had known Trigger and Mack from high school. They peeped me out in the lunch room one day banging on the table, battling a couple of seniors. In our high school lunch time was like freestyle Friday on 106th and Park. Trigger and Mack kept to themselves but they always took an interest in the battles during lunch. They were the type of dudes that just did their school work and went home; they didn't get involved in all the extra bullshit. A few days after I started battling everybody in school knew that I could spit and one day when I was in line waiting to pay for my food they approached me with an offer that I couldn't refuse. Of course I thought they were on some bullshit when they said they could get me studio time, after all they were just some regular high school kids like me. At first I just spent time in the studio watching other artist, then I started practicing my vocals and a few months later they had me doing verses on their tracks, with time I was dropping tracks on my own. Eventually I got signed to their label Jack in the Box. Every since I linked up with them my hobby became a career. If it weren't for them I would probably be working at some shitty dead end job busting my ass just to make ends meet, or in the streets waiting for my life to expire. Before meeting them I never took my music seriously, it was just something I was good at, that passed time but after seeing what I was actually capable of it pushed me to write on a serious note. Every since I've been working with them I eat, sleep, and shit music. It wasn't just a job it was a lifestyle, a lifestyle that kept me eating good.

Most rappers from Detroit were a one hit wonder and I figured out why, it isn't because they couldn't rap it's because Detroit doesn't really support its local rappers. Granted, alot of locals couldn't rap but that wasn't a reason to shoot every artist down, it was like the scenario that one spoiled apple ruined the whole bunch. Although we got mad love in the city we still did most of our concerts in other states and cities. We got love from people in the hood but we got more love from other states so we showed them our appreciation by having concerts and by releasing our music there first. The three of us had put too much time and money into our music to just let it flop because nobody wanted to see us on the come up but nonetheless we had creditability in Detroit. Detroit was our starting place and we held the city near and dear to our hearts but money talked and Detroit money just didn't speak loud enough.

Mack went into the booth," Alright nigga's stop squawking and let's get to work."

Mack was all about his money and so was I but he was like our father figure so he stayed on top of our heads making sure when we were in the studio we actually did some work instead of just smoking weed and talking shit. Mack made most of the beats and only rapped on one of our tracks occasionally but when either of us did a show he was always on stage first getting the crowd amped up before we came out to perform. Mack was good people he always looked out for me and Trigger, he kept us focused on what was important. We were like the three musketeers in the music world. For dudes like us music was really the only thing that was loyal. We couldn't trust females, and real friends were rare so we looked to music. Making music kept us all warm and fed. Music can't betray you or speak ill of you but it is without a doubt stressful. I loved rapping but a lot of my days got lost in the studio then again there was nothing that I would rather be doing other than having my hands wrapped around a mic. I can't even begin to count the amount of hours that I spent writing or trying to get my vocals on a track just right, I was more than dedicated.

I spent most of my time in the studio dropping actual tracks, I wrote the majority if not all of my songs at home. I had converted my basement into a studio so that I could work from home but either way I was always in the studio. I liked working in the studio at home because it was more of a challenge, I had to figure out what I was doing wrong instead of Mack or Trigger being my guide. I was about to hit the booth hard with a new song that I had written called, "On the Come Up." It was basically a story about how I started rapping and why I stayed true to music. Mack loved the heart that I put behind the song he didn't condone making music that other people couldn't relate to. It was one of those songs that everyone could relate to whether you were a rapper, mail man, or a doctor. It was a song for all the dreamers in the world who were struggling to make their dreams a reality; it was for all the hopefuls. I found it easier to rap about real shit opposed to trying to go hard about shit that I had never been through or done. A lot of rappers wanted to fabricate stories about how they were selling dope but I had seen so much in my life that I didn't have to make up stories or over exaggerate situations. Every time I dropped a track is was about something real, my motto was to educate people as well as to entertain them. Too many rappers were artificial; my goal was to breathe the life back into rap and hip hop. I always did interviews and the main question people wanted to know was what motivated my style of rap, my answer was always the same......Everything around me.

When I left the studio it was almost midnight. I had successfully finished the song and it was ready to be put on my album. The album that I was working on revolved around one theme. Every song had to do with following your dreams and setting your own bar. I was targeting younger people to let them know that there were more ways to get money than hustling on the block. I watched so many kids in my neighborhood waste their lives trying to chase a dollar or die trying, this album was for them. I used to be one of those little nigga's that thought money and females were all that mattered but if you spend enough time chasing the wrong things, it all will eventually catch up to you.

Chapter Two

After being in the studio all day I was hungry as hell so I hit Coney Island to get some wing dings and chili cheese fries, then hopped on the freeway to get to my crib before Trina. I had given her a key one night in an attempt to avoid an argument but I hated having her posted in my shit while I wasn't there. I had never known her to be a thief nor have people chilling while I wasn't home but in the same breath I didn't put it passed her ass or anyone else. As soon as I got to the crib I smashed my food watching sports high lights. I did a quick clean up of my place and jumped in the shower. As I was pulling my basketball shorts up, I heard her pull up blasting music in my driveway. I slapped some cologne behind me ears and headed to the door. I opened the door and there she was. I don't care what anybody said she was one of the prettiest females walking around the damn city. She was Puerto Rican and Black which was a turn on from jump street. Her skin was an almond brown color and was so damn smooth. She was about 5"9 with that whole coke bottle shape going on and ass for days. Her eyes were this really pretty light brown and they changed colors with the seasons. She defiantly was beautiful but beauty is only skin deep, beyond her physical attributes she didn't have much to offer. She embraced me with a hug smelling like another nigga's cologne, I thought to myself," bitch if you're going to cheat at least take a shower before you come over hugging on me", then I remembered she probably had been dancing up on some nigga for a little extra cash. One thing about her she wasn't cheap, if you wanted a dance from her at the club you had to break bread. I felt sorry for all the pitiful nigga's who spent all their hard earned money just to feel her ass clap on their lap, at the end of the night most of them left penniless with a hard dick.

She put her purse down and started kissing and sucking on my neck, I could feel my dick pressing against my shorts but before it got to its fullest potential I pulled myself back, "So how was work baby girl?"

She smiled," It was ok baby, same old tired ass brothers looking for something extra. I missed you though!"

There was that smile that could make a blind man fall in love, regardless of the shit she put me through, her smile could make up for it. She had perfect succulent lips and all her teeth were straight and white unlike most of the females I knew who had crooked teeth, off white or missing. Trina definitely took care of herself and made sure she was A-1 from head to toe.

We sat on the couch talking for a minute before her phone started ringing; out of respect I always turned my phone on silent when she was around so she had my undivided attention. Unlike me, her ringer was on full blast and she always answered it. She looked at the screen and her whole attitude changed. I went into the kitchen and fixed a glass of Patron while she took her little phone call. I could hear her voice but it was a faint whisper so I could only make out every other word of the conversation. I wasn't the noisy type but I was suspicious of who the hell was calling her so late. If it were my phone that was ringing she would have thrown a temper tantrum about who and why someone was calling me at almost two thirty in the morning. Women were funny with shit like that, they didn't want men asking them questions but they were always ready to interrogate a guy for the smallest thing. I learned a long time ago to just let the petty shit go because it wasn't worth the headache and you never would hear the end of it. I sat back down next to her and flicked through the channels just waiting for the excuse that she was about to give me.

"Well baby I have to go Kim and Drew had another fight and I have to go pick her up, you know how they get when they argue."

I laughed," You know what Trina, I can't do this shit any more. When you walk out this bitch don't come back. I'll drop your shit off tomorrow, and then were done."

I knew damn well it wasn't her friend Kim calling. Her dude had been on lock down for the past month, she thought I was stupid but I knew a lot of nigga's doing bids so I always knew when somebody was a caged bird or a free man. Her face told on her any way, when she first looked at her phone her whole attitude and facial expression changed. I can't stand liars but bad liars made it even worse, and she was the worse liar I had ever met but she was a creative with her tales. There is only so much a person can take before they haul off and snap, I had reached my breaking point. I already felt like a fool but I damn sure wasn't about to let her play me for one any longer. The cold confused expression on her face was priceless. I knew she was searching for something to do or say to make me change my mind but I really wasn't interested in listening.

She wrapped her arms around me," What do you mean were done?"

I removed her arms," I didn't stutter."

She started crying and grabbing her things. I had to laugh because it was funny; she was so dramatic about the situation. If anyone was going to cry it should have been me for putting up with all her deceitful ways. After all the shit she had put me through she thought I was going to break down and forgive her because she shed a few tears. I didn't understand females like her they get a man who is willing to do right by them, and then turn around and act a fool. I hadn't been perfect but I kept it real with her and in return that is all I expected. If she ever questioned why she wasn't my girlfriend, her present actions were a part of the reason. She could have been an award winning actress for the dramatic role she was playing.

Finishing my liquor, "Why the tears now?"

She snarled," Because nigga.......I'm pregnant with your fucken baby and you're talking about were done? Typical nigga shit. It's cool though mutha fucka......I don't need you or this shit."

Knowing her, anybody with a dick could have been the daddy. I didn't want her starting any shit waking up my neighbors so I just kissed her forehead, "Calm down shorty we will talk about it in the morning. Go get yah girl and I'll holla at you later."

She poked her lip out and dried her fake ass tears," Promise baby?"

I nodded," You know my word is bond."

She tossed me a smile and closed the door behind her.

I rolled up a blunt and thought to myself."I'm fucked."

Trina was one of those scandalous bitches; if you fucked her over she would shake your whole world up, I had enough problems so I didn't need any from her. I couldn't picture myself being the father of her baby, anything was possible but I didn't trust her enough to run up in her raw but we had broken a few rubbers during our sex escapades. I would have to play it safe and see what happened, if she really was pregnant, I wanted a paternity test to make sure the baby was mine. I wasn't a fool, I'd be damned if I sat up and took care of her child without first seeing if it was mine. Too many people I knew had gotten trapped into taking care of kids that weren't theirs and I wasn't about to be one of those fools. If the baby was mine then I would most defiantly take care of my responsibilities as a father but a baby wouldn't make me stay with Trina. As far as she and I went, baby or no baby, we were done, she could throw all the temper tantrums in the world and it wouldn't change a damn thing in my mind, we are done.

The next morning I had three missed calls two from Trina and one from Shawn. I wasn't worried about Trina at the moment so I hit Shawn up. It was too early in the morning to deal with her and I didn't want my morning starting off on a bad note. I figured, if you started your day off on the wrong foot it will end on the wrong foot. I planned on delaying talking to her at least until I had time to wash my ass, brush my teeth, and figure out what to say.

I dialed Shawn's number and the phone rang like three times before he shouted," Wad up doe nigggggggggga!"

Chuckling," What's the word bro?"

He sighed," This shit is about to trip you out bro. So last night Quan, Greg, and me hit the strip club. We were in that bitch posted when I looked up and saw Trina working some nigga a little too hard. He had his hands all up her skirt and shit. I thought I was buzzing so I dropped the line to Quan and he was like hell yeah that's her. I mean I know you drop a chick a few dollars and she will make dat ass clap but damn. So we finish up our drinks and get ready to hit the door then we see her walking out with Mike all hugged up like they were husband and wife."

I knew she had stepped back into her old ways but I didn't know she was getting down like that. This was the same nigga that smoked my weed and ate my food. I wasn't buddy…buddy with Mike but he was a dude I rolled with. We kicked it from time to time and played ball and went to the club sometimes on the weekends, the nigga was cool in my book. I didn't put anything pass anybody but it was still a shock. The same people you roll with are the same ones that will do the dirtiest things behind your back.

Digging through my closet," Word nigga?"

Shawn blurted," You know I got you. I bullshit you not them mutha fuckas walked out that bitch looking like Bonnie and Clyde or some shit."

I shook my head," Iight nigga good lookin but Im'a holla at you a little later."

I sat on my bed for a minute just thinking. After all the drama I decided to go see the one woman in the world who always knew what to tell me. I hopped in the shower, got dressed, and headed to my mama's crib. My mama is the one person that kept me sane and level headed. I coasted to her house listening to a few tracks that I did a while back. When I pulled up to her house she was in the garden tending to her tomato plants and greens, my mama loved working in the garden, growing up almost every vegetable we ate was home grown. I turned off the car and stepped out with a big smile on my face.

Before I could even make my way to where she was sitting I heard her loving voice shout," There's my baby!"

I chuckled," Hey mama!"

Embracing me in a hug," Now, help an old lady up! Are you hungry, I'll fix you some breakfast?"

I put a hand out and lifted her from the ground," Nah ma I'm straight ma."

Dusting her pants off," So what's wrong I can see it all on your face?"

That's one reason why I loved my mama she always knew when something was wrong, no matter how many times I told her I was fine she could see right through me. I guess that was a mother's job well a good mother's job any way, to know when something was wrong with their kids. It didn't matter if it was something as small as a headache, my mother could sense it. Her ability to see right through me was a blessing and a curse. Sometimes there were things I just didn't want my mother knowing but she always could sense a problem and wouldn't stop until I finally told her what was bothering me.

She placed her hand on my cheek," Baby, tell me what's going on. Anthony you know you can tell me anything, right?"

I took a deep breath, "Yes I know. You know that girl Trina I've been seeing, well she is pregnant and she claims it's mine. I swear she sleeps with too many people so who knows if it's mine or some other mans and on top of that we've never had sex unprotected but the condom did break a few times."

As soon as I let those words fall from my lips I knew my mama was about to cut into me. Although my mama was a God fearing Christian, she could get hood when she had to and she did so without hesitation. I loved the relationship we had because we always talked about everything from T.V to sex, we pretty much had an open relationship. Even though I could talk to her openly I still had to remember she was my mother and I needed to watch my attitude and language. Growing up under her roof respect was something you either gave or you got your ass beat.

Placing her hand over her mouth as if she was in shock," Baby I don't know why you put up with her and her nonsense. You are 22 years old, intelligent, kind hearted, successful and handsome but you tie yourself down to her and her foolish ways. I told you when you first started dating her to watch your back now she is pregnant all of a sudden? She is a stripper so I don't know why you laid down with her in the first place but I've never met the child so I can't pass judgment upon her. I can't tell you what to do but if that baby is yours, you already know that you will be a man and step up to the plate and take care of your responsibilities."

I looked down at my shoes," I know ma but something about her makes me stick around and you already know I handle mine."

She laughed," Boy if you don't stop talking to me like I'm one of your little friends, I'm going to pop you in the mouth. I know this is personal but if you know she sleeps around why do you even bother dealing with her?"

I didn't have an answer for her question. I knew she was blunt but damn she just threw salt on my wounds. That was a good question and honestly I was starting to wonder the same damn thing. I put myself in this position, so I was the only person who could get myself out of it. I knew I was messing around with a hoe but I continued to be with her for whatever reason. I guess I thought I could make her change but once a hoe always a hoe. It didn't matter why I chose to stay because she was all out of chances and life lines.

I looked through the mail on the table," Honestly ma, I don't know. In the heat of the moment I guess it just feels right. I guess I've been thinking with the head in my pants instead of the one on my shoulders. I hate to cut this visit short but I have to hit the studio. I will call you one day during the week to check up on you."

She grabbed my hand," Anthony whatever happens you're still my son and I know you'll do the right thing. Don't let what she can offer you sexually cloud your judgment on what is right and what is wrong. I love you."

I smiled," Your right mama and I won't. I love you too."

As I was walking away she shouted," And boy the next time you pull in my damn drive way you better not have that music so loud. You pulled up shaking the neighbor's windows; you better act like I raised you!"

I laughed," Yes mam.

When I pulled off I finally decided to call Trina to see what she was talking about. Her phone went straight to voice-mail. I threw my phone on the seat, shit I was kind of happy that she didn't answer. I pushed in my Raymond vs. Raymond C.D into the dash and got lost in my thoughts all the way back to my crib. I prayed to

God that she wasn't pregnant. I wanted kids but not by a chick like her. Shit you make your bed and you're bound to lay in it, I chuckled to myself that was one bed that I never wanted to rest my head in. I took being with her as a lesson learned, I would never go down that route with another female like her, they are more trouble than their worth, especially when the best thing they have to offer is sex. I needed to build my life with someone who had more to offer, I needed to stop being blinded by pussy.

Chapter Three

I pulled up to my crib and Trina's car was parked on the opposite side of the street and there was another car behind it. I recognized most of the cars on my street but not that one, plus it was pulled too close to Trina's. I closed the door to my truck and was on ten, more than ready to bust some body's head open. I eased my anger; maybe it was one of her friends helping her get her things. I burst through the door and looked around. Everything seemed to be in its right place, I stood still for a second and concentrated on the noises I heard coming from the direction of my bedroom. I crept towards the end of the hallway and pushed the door open. The door flung back and slammed against the wall, startling Trina as she was positing herself on top of Mike.

I shouted, "Bitch what the fuck?"

Mike looked up," Aww shit."

I went to my closest and grabbed my nine," Both of you mutha fucka's better be out of here before I start dropping bodies."

Trina screamed," Ant, calm down."

I put my finger on the trigger," Naw bitch. You and this bitch ass nigga better get the fuck out now."

I stood there griping my heat waiting for them to gather their shit and leave. Although they were both basically still fully clothed, if I hadn't walked in I'm sure they would have been naked enjoying each other's company a little too much.

I counted Five...Four...and before I got to Three they were running out the front door. That bitch had defiantly lost her mind coming in my house trying to fuck another dude in my bed. I was done with her ass, baby or no baby she was about to get wrote the fuck off. I felt like putting Mike and her nasty ass eight feet under but I had to get my head right before I did some dumb shit. Instead of sitting in the crib pouting like a bitch, I went to the studio to blow some steam off. I always hit the booth hard when I was mad. I pushed record and just let my emotions speak. For the first time in a while I went into the booth without having anything written, I wasn't the type to freestyle but today turned over a whole new leaf for me as artist. The anger I had in my heart told a story, I pushed stop and let the recording play back. Surprisingly, it was actually good, raw material, with a little tweaking and a hard ass beat, it would make a nice little track. After spending a few hours in the studio I had enough and decided to call my best-friend to see what she was doing. I hopped in the car and started to head home as I dialed Shay's number.

Her phone rang a few times before she picked up," Hey Ant!"

Just hearing her voice made me feel better," What's good Shay?"

She cleared her throat," Shit about to go to the mall and re-up on some clothes and shoes, you know I have to stay fresh!"

I laughed," Yeah, I know."

She giggled," Do you want to go? I need someone to carry all my bags!"

Smiling, "Yea, but I'm not carrying bags. I'll be there in fifteen or twenty minutes."

We hung up and I bust a U-turn and headed to her house. Shay was my first love but we ended up just being really good friends. We grew up together and we always had a soft spot for one another. She was the girl who I use to take baths with, the one who saw me in my spider man pajamas when I was six, we witnessed each other's most embarrassing moments from ass whippings to braces, we had seen it all. We had known each other our whole lives, every since we were kids I had a crush on her. She was the only female I had ever really looked at in a different light. She wasn't like other girls that I knew she was special. When I pulled up she walked out the house in her apple bottom outfit looking good as usual, she was the reason why red bones were red bones. She had long reddish brown hair that complimented her caramel complexion. When she smiled her dimples added to her beauty, she had one of those doll baby faces. As soon as she opened the door I could smell her perfume. She always wore Ed Hardy, which smelled extra right on her.

She closed the door and kissed me on my cheek," Hey big head!" I smirked," What up short stack."

I always called her short stack because she was taller than most women but when she stood next to me she looked like a child. I started calling her that in middle school and it just stuck.

We drove to the mall listening to some Jeezy just laughing at little bullshit enjoying each other's company. When she was with me she didn't have to pay for anything. I stopped at the bank and withdrew a couple of stacks from my account and I had my credit cards just in case I didn't get enough cash. Money wasn't an object when it came to her; we both always wore the best of the best. I wasn't a flashy person but I liked nice things, plus I bust my ass to get them. We stepped inside the mall and it seemed like all eyes were on us. Most females gave her evil looks and most guys checked me from head to toe, nigga's wanted her and bitches wanted me. We walked side by side serving each other justice. We went to several stores and I cashed out on whatever she put on the counter regardless of the price tags. Shay was high maintenance but she could carry her own I just was in the habit of spoiling her. When we left the mall we went to Friday's which is where we usually ended up since it was her favorite place to eat. We got a table next to the window and ordered some shots, while we waited for our drinks I told her about the shit with Trina and Mike, along with the pregnancy. It wasn't a surprise to her then again I guess it wasn't a surprise to me either but damn in my house, in my bed, is what had me gone off my rocker.

She shook her head," They both had balls for that shit especially Mike because that nigga goes into bitch mode any time you raise your voice."

Shay didn't give a fuck she cut into any and everybody if they were in the wrong. That is what I liked most about her, most females would sit up and sugar coat shit but she dished everything out exactly how she saw and thought it. She was intelligent and could back up everything that she said. I could tell her anything and she would listen, even if she didn't want to hear or care about what I was saying, she would just listen. The waitress brought our drinks and took our order. I ordered our favorite appetizers potatoes skins and hot wings, to hold us over until the food came. Shay was a nice size but she could put away some food, most of the time we would argue over who got the last wing or potato skin.

She put her drink on the table," Sweetie you can do so much better than that trick. Your music has taken off and you're going places but she has you stuck. Stop thinking with your dick, that's what's keeping you. I know her pussy game must be cold but it's not worth the drama. No pussy in this world is worth all the shit she drops on you. "

Shay cut into me with no remorse. Shit, she was right Trina did have some of the best pussy I ever had but that wasn't a good reason to stick around. Females with a good sex game came a dime a dozen. I was just mesmerized by her shit and it didn't help that she had no limits when it came to sex. We definitely had shared some wild times between the sheets, sex was my weakness and I had no shame in admitting it. Shay had a way of laying everything out and putting it in perspective for me, it was time for me to wise up.

I wiped my face," Man I can't even act like you aren't saying some real shit but it goes deeper than that, well at-least I would like to think it does. I know I have to let her go because if I don't I'm going to end up doing a bid for putting her and these nigga's she fucks in the ground."

Shay damn near choked from laughing," Now best-friend you can't hold a nigga up for getting pussy from a bitch who's throwing it like a free for all. Don't chase the dudes tackling that ass because it's human nature. If she has a crumb snatcher and it's yours you know what you need to do but other than that don't even get involved with that brawd. Bitches like that will take you for everything that you have, don't even give her the

39

opportunity."

Laughing, "Yeah your right about that. I just don't understand some females they want a good dude but when they get one then they don't know how to act. "

Smiling," Maybe you're just messing with the wrong females, you need a woman not a little girl playing dress up."

Talking to Shay brought back so many memories. I missed being with her. She was a real down ass female and I never had to worry about her cheating. I couldn't even remember why we stopped talking like we used to but now I understand that at the time when we did date I wasn't ready for a relationship but now I'm older and wiser. Shay had so much to offer she was intelligent, funny, beautiful, honest, easy to talk to, and had goals. Females having goals was rare. She was the type of woman that made you question whether or not you even deserved her. We finished our food and drinks and sat there for a while just talking. I felt better after talking to her and putting everything out in the open.

I went to pull my wallet out and she put her hand out," Nope, I got this!"

Shaking my head," Nah...I got it."

When we left the restaurant I dropped her off and headed to my crib. I got home and laid on the couch to watch T.V. , I was half way sleep when the door bell rang.

I shouted," Who is it?"

I hated people coming to my house unannounced like it was Grand Central Station or some shit. The only person I ever expected to pop up unannounced was my mama but even she called before coming over. I felt like it was rude to just go over someone's house without calling. I turned off the T.V and dragged myself to the door.

The voice on the other end of the door spoke," It's me baby......Trina."

I got up and opened the door," What the fuck do you want girl?"

The next thing I know a nigga shot me twice with a 38. I instantly felt the sting of the bullets. I didn't know what was going on, what type of nigga knocks on your door to shoot you. My body seemed heavier than usual, everything was just dead weight. Being shot immediately makes you feel like you're going to go see Jesus, everything was in slow motion as I dropped to the floor.

I heard a familiar voice," Nigga don't you ever pull a gun on somebody unless you plan on using it."

I felt light headed and the room seemed brighter than usual, I tried to pull myself up but it was no use. I'm 6'5 and 220 lbs so trying to pull myself up from the floor with two bullets in me was false hope. Luckily my neighbor heard the gun shots and called the police. I lived in a semi decent neighborhood so gun shots were unusual unlike in the hood where they were familiar like doorbells.

The elderly woman inched her way over my lawn making sure danger wasn't present," Child are you alright?"

I wanted to say," BITCH NO I just got shot", but I held my composure, "I'll be alright Ms. Washington."

She tried to help me up but her brittle bones couldn't handle my weight," I called 911, they should be here soon."

I managed to grab the door knob and lift myself up. When the police came they asked me if I knew who it was, I lied and said no. I didn't know who shot me but I had an idea that it was Mike. He was the number one suspect in my mind. I had something special for him and Trina's ass. If she thought she could just have someone try to take me out the game and get away with it, the bitch had another thing coming. The EMS arrived and put an oxygen mask on me and gave me some pain medication. I must have passed out because when I woke up I was in a room by myself with the lights out. I just laid there looking out the window at the stars. The hospital kept me for three days to monitor my condition but I wasn't hurt too bad one bullet went through my shoulder and the other one was in my chest, I was lucky because it damn near pierced my heart.

When I was released from the hospital I was down for a few weeks. Shawn and Shay kept a close eye on me and made sure I had what I needed. My mom went ballistic when she heard what happened but after Shawn dropped word that I was going to be alright and Shay assured her that she was taking great care of me, she kind of calmed down. My mama visited me almost every day and brought me pies, cakes, and other desserts. I felt like a kid again, I wasn't use to people catering to me. I wasn't a bitch nigga but I wasn't stupid either. I didn't know if the shooter would return so Shawn spent a couple of nights just in case. He parked his car in the garage so it would appear that I was alone. Shawn and I both knew that this was a start to a fight that would only end in bloodshed. Neither of us was about to drop the situation and just let it be water under the bridge. We weren't the type of dudes to take things like getting shot lightly. Somebody would pay for my wounds; that's just the way things worked out where me came from.

Shawn bit down into his sandwich," You know I'll take whoever shot you out. I don't care if it was Mike or somebody else; just say the word and I'll dump a few clips into their ass. Shit I'll dump Trina's ass in a ditch nobody will miss her but the nigga's that go to the club to see her shake that ass. Hoes like her are easily replaced."

I laughed that shit off, Shawn was crazy and I didn't want him doing anything stupid that would cost both of us our freedom. I wasn't sure what I was going to do but whatever it was I was going to handle it myself. Shawn would take a bullet for me and I would do the same for him but this was something I wanted him to stay out of for the time being. Sometimes Shawn didn't think things through and would just haul off and do something dumb. I liked to plan my moves out and execute them with some kind of order, the last thing I wanted to do was make the situation any sloppier. I was still weak so there wasn't anything I could do any time soon and besides if we started shooting up people the police would automatically be beating down my door.

Fixing my pillow," No, for now we will let nigga's breathe."

Shawn left to go chill with one of his chicks, Shay stayed over to keep me company. We watched T.V. for a minute until things got a little heated. One thing led to another and the next thing I know she was kissing on my neck and had her hands on my dick. I couldn't help the urge to want to make love to her. All that best-friend shit was out the window. I wanted to take my time with her and satisfy her every need. She was special and I wanted to treat her right.

She kissed my lips then whispered in my ear," Do you want me daddy?"

I looked in her eyes and slowly started undressing her. She smelled like fresh strawberries which only made my dick thirst for her even more. Once I removed all her clothes I enjoyed the view of her erect nipples and beautiful body. One minute we were kissing and the next she had my dick sliding in and out her mouth. When she was done I sat her down on my face and let her juices quench my thirst. We both laid there in pleasure. She climbed on top of my dick and we went into pure ecstasy. My phone was ringing off the hook but I didn't give a fuck. Our bodies were intertwined and nothing else matter at that moment. The pain from my wounds didn't even matter; I was lost in the moment.

She rode my dick like she was going to win a cash prize," Oooow Ant I'm about to cum."

I could feel her pussy muscles squeezing around my dick," I'm ready baby."

The way her cum slid down my dick was in sync with the way my cum squirted inside her pussy. We laid there breathing like two dogs in heat. I never expected us to make love but I was glad it happened, everything felt so right.

She smiled and kissed me," Ant, I never stopped loving you. I've always wanted to be the one for you but over the years things changed."

I couldn't hide my feelings," I never stopped loving you either Shay."

I knew our friendship had always had its ups and down but the love we had for each other never changed. We talked for a while until we fell into a peaceful sleep. When we woke up Trina was standing over us. I thought it was a dream until I felt Shay clinched onto me like a leech. It was like scene from a moving the way she was just standing there looking at us.

I rubbed my eyes unsure of what I was seeing," Trina what are you doing here? You think you can still stroll up in this bitch after you had your new nigga shoot me up in my own spot?"

I wasn't expecting an answer because those were rhetorical questions. She had to be out of her God given mind if she thought she and I still had something going on.

She looked like she had been crying," I knew you was still fucken this bitch. All that shit you were talking about me stepping out on you and

47

fucking these other nigga's but you got her ass in this mutha fucka playing house."

I had to laugh at her psychotic ass," Don't start with me Trina. You have major issues, REAL TALK. You need to leave now."

Shay laid there holding on to me like a child that was having a nightmare. I had my gun under the couch just in case Trina tried some shit, I wasn't worried but I was prepared and wouldn't hesitate to grab my shit just in case. I stood up and put my shirt on.

Trina wiped her eyes," I just came to get the rest of my stuff and drop your key off."

I nodded," Well hurry up, your welcome has already been worn out."

She giggled," Oh, don't worry bastard I wouldn't want to be here with you and your new bitch any longer than I have to."

I whispered for Shay to go in the bathroom, I didn't trust Trina after that bullshit she pulled, if something did happen I didn't want Shay to be around to see it. For all I knew Trina had some dude waiting outside to blow me away. One thing about females like Trina they always had some nigga wrapped around their finger ready to do anything for them. After a few minutes Trina finally had all her shit and she gave me my key. I watched her walk to her car and drive away. I knocked on the door for Shay to come out.

She was crying," I was so scared baby. I thought she was going to kill me."

I wiped her tears," I would never let her hurt you."

Chapter Four

Three weeks later I was finally back on my feet. After spending so much time in the house I decided to hit the block. Word had already hit the streets that Trina was pregnant but nobody knew who the daddy was. Everybody was standing in line to clear their name from the list. I wasn't worried about it. I knew when the time came if the baby was mine I would sit her down and we would talk. I had other shit on my mind besides her and her bastard child. Shawn kept an eye on Mike because he was the number one suspect in my mind but the bitch got scared and went to stay with his brothers on the other side of town. I kicked it on the block for a minute with my cousin until him and his baby mama got to arguing. I wasn't trying to be around them and their crazy love affair. One minute they were arguing and the next they were ready to sex each other's brains out. I never understood shit like that but their relationship wasn't meant for me to understand.

My phone buzzed in my pocket as I backed out his drive way," Wad up nigga?"

Shawn turned his music down," Man let's go get this nigga right now. He is at his mama's crib."

That was the difference between Shawn and me, he was cold hearted. I would never run up on a nigga while he was chilling with his moms. Shawn didn't care; he would kill a nigga while he was taking a shit if he crossed his path. The streets had did him dirty over the years and it showed. I didn't even want to kill the little punk ass bitch, I just wanted to blow him a new ass hole and let him know who he was fucking with. I wasn't even sure if he was the one who pulled the trigger but he is the only nigga that had a reason to, so that was enough proof for me. I wasn't about to fight a nigga over a bitch especially one like Trina if he wanted her he could have her. Pussy came in by the bus load, I would never duke it out over some. I didn't trust people but being shot and not knowing who did it, really raised my eyebrow with suspicion.

Rolling down the windows, "Nah man lay low. We will catch up to him sooner or later."

I could hear Shawn's frustration," Iight man."

The line went dead......

I went to check on Shay and spend some time with her. I knew she was still a little shaken up and I wanted to make sure she was alright. One minute we were laughing and the next minute my phone was going nuts. I looked at the screen it was Quan. I hesitated to answer but he rarely called me so I knew something was up.

I answered, "Nigga what's the problem?"

He hesitated, "Shawn just shot up this nigga's mama's house."

I shouted," What nigga? I just talked to that nigga and told him to lay low. FUCK......"

Quan paused," Man you know how that nigga is, he's fucken trigger happy. The only thing I know is you need to roll thru the spot so we can figure out what the fuck to do."

I hung up the phone.

Kissing Shay on the cheek," I gotta be ghost for a minute baby."

She grabbed my shirt," Be careful baby."

I smiled," You know I'm going see you later."

She tossed me a cute little smile," You better!"

I hopped in the range and did about 90 all the way to Quan's spot. Shawn was my nigga but he didn't know how to listen, regardless of who pulled the trigger where we come from every mutha fucka involved could and probably would go down for the shit. The legal system is fucked up but locking nigga's like us up wasn't shit, nobody cared if some street nigga's got sent away, guilty or not. I wasn't about to go to prison for some dumb shit especially some shit that I didn't do, the day they locked me up and tossed away the key would be the day hell froze over. I pulled up to Quan's crib as soon as I got out the car these fools came outside gassed up. I was frustrated with Shawn but Quan irritated me how he was always egging Shawn on to do stupid shit. I really didn't care for Quan but he was Shawn's boy so he automatically became one of my boys too. We occasionally would shoot pool or blow a blunt but we weren't buddy, buddy with one another.

Shawn laughed," Man, I lit that nigga's shit up. I laid somebody out. Somebody sure the hell isn't bouncing back tonight."

Part of me wanted to slap the shit out of the nigga but the other part of me felt bad for him. Shawn never had a mama and his daddy dedicated his life to the streets. He had raised himself so he didn't have any remorse for other people and their feelings. It was like he didn't have a soul. All of his brothers were killers or drug dealers so he followed in their footsteps. My mama tried to keep him walking in the right direction but peer pressure is a big nasty bitch. She could only do so much and eventually got fed up with his nonsense, she never gave up on him but it's hard to encourage someone who has given up on themselves. Shawn looked at his brother's lives and he didn't see why his should be any different. He was a product of his environment. I hated to say it but it was only a matter of time before he ended up dead or in jail. I didn't like the crowd he ran with but he was my boy so I would never turn my back on him.

I leaned against the car," Man calm down. What the fuck happened, I told you to let that shit ride."

Quan laughed," Nigga that's like telling a hoe not to suck dick.......It's not gone happen."

Shawn glared at him," Dog, shut the fuck up but naw Ant, I was chillen on the block with Ashley and I heard these little young nigga's talking about how Mike was laid up in your bed with Trina. I grabbed the burner and just went dumb on that fool and whoever else was posted in the cut with him."

I shook my head," You just couldn't fucken listen. I specifically told you to lay low."

Shawn sucked his teeth," Oh so you're going to nut up on your boy now, I was watching your fucken back and this is how you gone act nigga?"

Quan looked confused," So fuck the bullshit, what are we gone do?"

Shawn dusted his shoes off," I don't know what yall are gonna do but I'm far from worried a dude like me been at his worst, nobody is going keep me down."

I opened the car door," Nigga that is your problem. I'll call you when I figure some shit out. Lay low and don't' say shit about shooting up his mama's house. The two of you need to go do something constructive."

Shawn flung his hand in the air," Yea ok."

I jumped in the car and left them nigga's in the rear view. I had a million thoughts going through my head. What if his stupid ass shot up his mama or his sisters? Everybody knew we had it out for the nigga so all the fingers pointed at us. I had to figure out something and I had to do it fast before any more problems were caused. My mama raised me to defend myself but she also raised me to know when to walk away. I had enough money I was ready to say fuck it and pack my shit up and move to Mexico. I was tired of the drama. I wouldn't dare step foot on Mike's block because it was too hot. Even if Shawn didn't kill anybody, I already knew we all had tags on our heads. Mike was a cup cake ass nigga but he had plenty of nigga's who would gladly do his dirty work. I sat at a stop light thinking, all this bullshit started over Trina. Her nasty ass caused more problems than she was worth. No woman was worth this much trouble. When the light turned green I zoomed off down Evergreen to my brother's house. My brother Tone was a real street nigga who always knew what the streets were talking about so I already knew he would have the word on what went down at Mike's. When I pulled up to his house he was working on his car. Tone went to school for automotive technology but he never finished, it didn't make a difference because he could still work miracles under the hood.

"Aye." I yelled out.

He lifted his head from the hood," Haaaaa,wad up doe lil bro."

"Nothing bro trapped in this bullshit." I shrugged.

Tone laughed," So I heard. That bitch Trina got nigga's going wild."

Searching for my lighter," Hell yeah. I know you heard about that shit with Mike."

Closing the car hood," Yeah I heard ya boy Shawn lost his mind and shot his mama's house up. That shit was pointless, everybody was outside and shit. He killed a couple of couch pillows and a picture that's about it. You know you have to end the shit before that nigga ends you, right?"

Lighting up a blunt," Straight, that nigga was talking like he sprayed blood. I know one thing I'm tired of this back and forth tit for tat shit."

We sat in the range smoked a couple of blunts and talked about how I was going to eliminate all my problems. I wasn't trying to get Tone involved because he already had two strikes if it wasn't for double jeopardy he would have three strikes and be in for life. I didn't want to see my brother in prison for the rest of his life but he was going to ride out with me regardless. Tone taught me everything I knew about the streets. No matter how hard our mama tried to keep us out the streets and away from violence we managed to end up there anyway. I only diverted my attention to the streets when I wasn't working on my music and that wasn't very often. Tone on the other hand lived for the streets. The streets had been good to him. My other brother had been killed trying to run the streets so I think that is what made Tone into the beast that he was. He was smart but he was ignorant, he didn't know when enough was enough. Getting money was all he lived for. I hated to say it but the streets would be the cause of his demise probably sooner than later. Nigga's like us have an expiration date.

I felt my phone vibrating, I looked at the screen it was Shay.

I passed the blunt back to Tone," Hey baby."

I could hear breathing but she wasn't saying anything.

I cleared my throat," Hello?"

A man's voice blared through the phone," You tried to have ya little puppet take my family out huh? You think you can punk me nigga?

Your girl Shay has some nice ass pussy, you just can't keep a bitch for shit. You can tell your boy Shawn that his life is over, believe that nigga."

Silence filled my ears.

Tone hit the blunt," Damn nigga who was that, they got you lookin twisted."

I put my phone down," I gotta bounce bro."

Tone lifted up his shirt revealing his burner," Nah I'm riding with you lil bro."

I backed out the drive-way and damn near ran every red light on the way to Shay's house. I pulled in her drive-way and was half way out of the car before I threw it in park. Her door had been kicked in. My heart was racing a mile per minute. I didn't know what to expect when I stepped into the house. I called her name what seemed like a million times as I checked her house inch by inch. I finally found her naked balled up in the corner of the kitchen.

Tone rushed up behind me," Damn."

I dropped to my knees and grabbed her face," Who did this to you?"

Tear rushed down her face," He raped me and said he was going to kill you and any other nigga that runs with you."

Tone blurted out," Who? "

I took my shirt off and put it over her head," Who?"

Wiping her eyes," I was getting dressed when I heard someone knock on the door. When I came downstairs to see who it was no one was there. I was walking back upstairs and the next thing I know Mike kicked the door in. I tried to run up the stairs but........."

I wrapped my arms around her," It's okay baby take your time."

She rested her head on my shoulders," He grabbed my leg and pulled me back down. I kept kicking him and kicking him and finally got loose. I was trying to get to the phone and call the police but he hit me and pushed me down to the floor. I kept screaming but nobody came. I kept kicking and screaming but he put a gun to my head and said he would shoot me if I didn't shut up. I was scared so I did what he said. He ripped my clothes off and raped me."

She cried even harder once she finally told me what happened," Baby it's going to be okay."

I sent Tone upstairs to get her some pants and shoes. My head was pounding; I was beyond pissed and hurt. Seeing Shay like that really hurt me. I helped her get dressed, she couldn't stop shaking, I picked her up and put her in the backseat of the car. I rummaged through the trunk to find another shirt, Tone jumped in and we drove straight to my mama's house. I wanted to take her to the hospital but she didn't want to go. When we got to my mama's house I didn't tell her what was going I just let her know that I needed her to let Shay rest her head there for a while until I came back. My mama tried to stop me and Tone from walking out the door because she knew we were at the point of no return...........

I hated seeing my mama upset.

She cried out," Please, don't go get into any trouble."

We didn't look back we just kept walking. I heard Shay call my name, I wanted to turn around but I knew if I turned around I wouldn't leave. I wanted to embrace her and promise her that everything was going to be okay but I couldn't let my emotions take over me I had to handle the shit before it spiraled any further out of control. We peeled out the drive-way and went back to my house; I had so many doubts going through my head nothing was clear. I let a bitch get inside my mind and take control; I let her have an effect on so many people in my life. It's wild as hell because before Trina, Mike and I were boys. Bitches like Trina fuck anybody over as long as their getting what they want in the process. I looked at the picture of Shay in my phone and at that second I decided the shit was over. Either I lived or Mike did but in the end both of us wouldn't be breathing or at least we wouldn't be breathing without assistance. I had never laid anybody to rest but I was going to do what I had to do. Nigga's respected me and they respected my hustle plus they already knew that if anything happened to me, Tone would deal with them personally. I always knew that sooner or later all the dirt I did would catch up to me, in the streets eventually every nigga pays their dues in blood or money.

Tone broke my train of thought," light lil bro enough of the bullshit. Are we going to do this or not?"

I grabbed all the clips I had in a shoe box that was wedged in the corner of my closet," Yea."

I went to call Shawn when Tone snatched the phone out my hand.

Tone shook his head," Peep game bro. Yah home boy Quan is sniffing Mike's ass heavy as hell. Him and Shawn are cool right? How the fuck do you think Mike knows so much about you? You and Mike were cool but only on occasion. Quan has spent a nice amount of time with you because he is with Shawn the majority of the time. Mike and Shay know each other but Mike never knew where she lived but Quan does. How do you think that nigga knew when you were home and when you would be alone? Trina has been feeding him your where about's. Why do you think that nigga punched your number in his phone the second Shawn popped off on ol boys house? Shawn is street smart but he never connected the dots, Quan has been using Shawn all along."

I scratched my head in confusion," Exactly what are you saying bro?"

Chapter Five

Tone sat on the edge of my bed," All three of them have been playing you from the start. Mike never fucked Trina it was all a part of the game. Trina is Quan's bitch all of that shit about Trina and Mike being hugged up and fucking was just for show. It's all been a game and you are the main playing piece. Remember when we stayed on LaSalle and you used to kick it with that little shorty, Kyrah?"

I sat on the other end of the bed," Lay this shit out for me bro because it isn't making sense but yea I remember her."

Tone pulled a picture out his pocket," First of all Kyrah is Mike's little sister."

I couldn't believe the shit I was hearing. I remembered Kyrah. She did have a big brother but I never met him. Most of the time we were at my house or she would sneak me in when everyone was sleep. We had sex a few times then I chucked up the deuces on her ass. I was young and stupid back then; I dogged pretty much every female that was willing to let me have sex with them. Shortly after I stopped talking to her we moved and I never talked to her again but everybody on the block said once I moved she started messing around with females. I never heard anything about her being pregnant but back then even if I had, I probably wouldn't have believed that the baby was mine.

Tone looked at me," I was at the club talking to one of the girl's at the bar. I dropped that bitch a stack and she told me everything I wanted to know. I didn't know who Trina was so I asked ole girl to point her out. When she showed me who she was I knew that I recognized her from somewhere but it took me a minute to put two and two together. This chicken head started telling me about some nigga that Trina had been playing for this guy Mike. She told me how sometimes Mike, Trina and another guy would go into the back of the club and talk big business."

I stopped that nigga in mid sentence," What the fuck?"

Tone walked over to the window," I asked her what the other guy looked like, she took me to the back and opened Trina's locker and showed me a picture, the picture of this infamous guy was Quan. Quan is the one who shot you. You said the voice sounded familiar, you were so sure it was Mike but it wasn't. You pulled a gun on Quan's girl and he wasn't having that shit."

I sat on the bed feeling like a fool. Everything slowly started to fall together in my head. Quan was the main one always egging me on about Trina, he stayed dick sucking Shawn and that nigga did know a little too much about me. For them to be a bunch of bitch ass nigga's they had my ass on a short leash. I felt like punching a hole through the wall. All this time I was laid up with Trina, she was Quan's woman. Shawn and I were both clueless about the clowns we kept around us and the shit they were doing. I felt so stupid but at the same time I was ready to put all three of those conniving bitches in the morgue.

Tone came back and sat on the bed," As far as I'm concerned it's me and you from now on. If you tell Shawn anything he will have all of us serving life for murder. We have to handle this shit ourselves. It's us against them, that's the way it should have been from the beginning. They've had the upper hand for a while; it's about time that you got bumped to the number one spot. I know Shawn is your boy but you can't let him know the deal with Quan."

I was ready to do whatever, I wanted all them mutha fucka's sucking food from a tube, especially Quan. I was confused about one thing, what made Tone go to the club and drop lines to the girl at the bar. I always talked about Trina and the stunt's that she pulled but up until recently he didn't know anything about the whole situation with Mike. He didn't know I got shot until my mama called him. I was close to Tone but there were still certain secrets that rested between us.

I looked over at Tone," Bro how did you figure all this shit out?"

He stood up and grabbed the blunt from behind his ear," I did a bid with Mike a few years back and he was talking about some nigga that fucked over his sister. I was just talking shit about how you and me use to fuck all the hoes in the hood and didn't give a fuck about their feelings. He got to talking about his youngest sister "Kyrah" and at the time I wasn't thinking, I was like my lil bro turned a little freak named Kyrah out. He pulled out a picture of him and her. I didn't say anything when he showed me the picture, but that was confirmation enough. I just kept my mouth shut and let him talk, I figured he was just holding onto some pent up aggression."

I shook my head," So are you telling me that you snitched on me nigga? You always talk about people talking too much but look at you."

Tone's faced dropped," I'm not a snitch bro. I didn't snitch; I didn't know he was on some revenge shit either. In the pin that's all you have to keep you going are stories about what the fuck you did when you were free. I swear I didn't know that nigga was plotting on you, until he showed me the picture I didn't even know we were talking about the same female. I didn't figure it out until I saw Trina. In the pin she was always paying that nigga visits but they never showed one another any sort of affection so I figured she was family or some shit. The other night I was up at Deja Vu tipping the freaks when I spotted her posted in the corner talking to Mike. I didn't know that the same bitch paying him visits was the same bitch you were laying your head with."

I couldn't even be mad. I had never been locked up for a long period of time; I never knew what it was like to live off hope. The longest bid I ever did was a year for possession when I used to sell a few rocks. My mind was blown away, this meant they had been planning shit on me for months, getting me deeper into their tangled web. Now I understood why Trina met eyes with me at the club it was all a set up. I knew the world was a ruthless place but damn I felt so small and I had never been so confused. The signs were obvious once Tone laid out all the pieces, I'll admit, I was impressed by their little scheme.

I cleared my throat," This nigga has had me wrapped around his finger, why start shit now? He could have been put me under."

Tone nodded," Mike got released a few weeks before me and I figured he had let that shit go. If I would have known he was plotting all of this I would have been punched that nigga's clock. One of my boys on the block said his sister had a baby and word got out that it was yours. You already know word on the street travels fast, He must have gotten wind that Trina was pregnant and heard how you were talking about taking care of the baby and her. I guess the nigga just flipped his top knowing that you were going to take care of some hoes baby but you left his sister out to dry. Getting Trina pregnant gave Quan even more motive to take you out the game and agree to Mike's plan. So the small time scheme of just getting money for Kyrah and her baby turned into a plan to put you six feet under."

Shaking my head," So that's why Trina wouldn't let me take care of her she was putting my money in that nigga's pocket to fund his sister and her baby."

Nodding," Yup, all for his sister."

I sat there thinking about every woman that I had ever fucked over, nobody ever told me anything about being pregnant. Yeah, I was stupid and didn't give a fuck about women but I wouldn't dare let my seed grow up in this world without me. I had seen a lot of pussy in my 22 years of living. I was young when I met Kyrah and I didn't know the effect of my actions. I didn't care about females or their feelings back then, I was ruthless. She never told me anything about being pregnant, but then again I booked up on her so fast she didn't even have the chance to. Shay was the first person to make me realize how special some females were, she was the only one to make me wait to be with her. She was the only one who didn't give a fuck about my money or what I could do for her. I thought about her and I thought about how over protective I was of my sisters and mama. It didn't matter how grimy a female was they deserved respect just like the respect I showed my mama and Shay but it's hard to respect someone who doesn't respect themselves. Thinking about the whole situation made me regret my actions but all this sad song shit wasn't going to stop me from putting a bullet between somebody's eyes.

I shook my head," So Trina is Quan's girl and Mike did all this just to get some money out of me for his sister and her baby. He could have just stepped to me and told me what was up. I know I was a bitch nigga back then, but I'm not the same little boy I was."

Tone blew smoke into the air and passed me the blunt, "Yup that is his chick and if I was Mike that would have been the smart thing to do but this is just twisted. It has become a game for these nigga's."

Although the whole plan was fucked up, it made perfect sense. I would have went crazy if someone got one of my little sisters Tasha or Asia pregnant and dipped but I would have corrected the error in a better manner. What made matters worse was I didn't leave Kyrah with a baby to take care of intentionally, word of me having a child was a bigger shock to me than the mess they pulled. I never realized how much of an ass I was until that moment.

Tone got up," It's now or never."

I agreed. I was tired of being their puppet, it was time for the curtain on their little show to close. We got up and headed for the living room, when a knock at the door stopped us both in our tracks........

I already hated when people showed up at my door unannounced but with all the recent events unannounced visits put me on edge. I had already been shot at my crib that wasn't about to happen again. I walked over to the door with my hand clinched on the trigger of my 9.This time I was ready for Quan, Mike, or any other bitch nigga that tried to run up on me. I looked out the window and saw a girl holding a little boy.

Tone shouted," Who is it bro?"

Shrugging my shoulders," Shit I don't know some chick with a kid."

The girl looked familiar but I couldn't figure out why. I swear I had seen her somewhere before but I couldn't put my finger on it. I figured she just resembled somebody that I knew. I tucked my gun away because I didn't see her as a threat.

I opened the door," Sorry sweetheart I think you have the wrong house."

She put the little boy down," No, your Anthony right?"

I nodded," Yea, whose asking?"

She laughed," Damn do I look that different? It's me Kyrah. I asked around and finally found out where you lived."

My brain was stuck on stupid, I didn't know what to say. Here I was face to face with the girl who was affected by my dirty ways. I was expecting her to slap me or start yelling and create a scene for all my neighbors to see but she didn't. She had the sweetest smile on her face and was very calm. She was right, I didn't recognize her.

She cleared her throat," This is Christopher.......Your son."

When I heard those words I wanted to play bitch and disown the idea of him being mine but one look at him and I knew he was my son. He had the same little shy look I had when I was his age. His eyes were big and bright just like mine. Everything about him screamed me. Even though he resembled me you could defiantly tell who his mother was as well. It was amazing how he was a spitting image of us both.

I stood aside," Come in and chill for a minute."

She agreed," Ok but we can't stay long I have to take him to my mom's house before I go to work."

Once Tone saw that everything was cool he slipped into my room. I could hear the TV and him laughing, I knew he had made himself at home. I sat there for the longest trying to do anything I could to avoid conversation but finally she broke the silence," It's been a long time, how have you been?"

Disregarding her question," Why didn't you tell me that you were pregnant?"

Placing Christopher on the couch next to her," Ant, neither of us were ready for a child back then and I knew you weren't a family man. I was 17 when I got pregnant, I was confused and hurt. You just up and left, there was no need to bother you. I just came here to make peace with you so my brother would lay off the situation. I don't need your money and I don't want your sympathy. I never asked my brother to do any of this. I've been hearing about all the madness and I want it to stop before anybody else gets hurt."

I tugged on my shirt to loosen the wrinkles," I feel you. Regardless of the games I played with you, you were pregnant with my seed and I would have taken care of the both of you. I know I played a lot of games back then but I'm not that same person and I've missed out on three years of my son's life because of that bullshit. Whatever beef your brother and I have won't stop because of this conversation but I'm glad you came. All of this is a shock to me and I think we need to get together and talk about it."

I could see the hurt in her eyes. I could hear it in her voice, she was fighting back tears. She was an independent woman but I could tell that life had hit her hard. She wasn't the same girl I fucked over. She was a fearless woman now. She looked good. Her dark brown skin looked radiant, she had gained some weight but that didn't take away from her beauty. I examined her and Christopher. His clothes and shoes were new and he had a fresh cut. There was no doubt that they both were doing fine without my help. I couldn't change the past but I knew that from now on I would play a part in both of their lives. I wanted to get to know my son and I wanted to make up with Kyrah and show her how sorry I was for not being there for them.

Biting her bottom lip," Anthony I appreciate that. I just wanted to clear the air. This little feud has gone on long enough. I want you to be in your son's life because I want him to know who his daddy is but I don't want you to be in his life because you feel obligated. I've managed to provide for us this long so I will understand if you don't want to be a part of his life. It's foolish of me to think I can stop this bullshit by coming to visit you but I just hope it drenches the fire between you guys, this shit has gotten way out of hand."

I didn't reply, I was stuck in the moment.

She scribbled her number down on a piece of paper," When and if you're ready to talk......Call me."

She kissed me on the cheek and just like that she and Chris were gone. My trance was broken when Tone charged into the living room," So nigga are we going to ride or what? My little shorty is waiting for me at the crib."

My mind was wrapped up on some other shit I wanted to see Mike and

Quan tap out but at the same time maybe Kyrah was right. All this time we had been slithering through the grass unknowingly because of her. All this drama was declared on her behalf but it wasn't upon her request. I could understand Mike's frustrations with me because I was a big brother as well but Quan had put his own spin on the already fucked up situation. I could even understand him wanting me dead but I couldn't understand why he chose to play cat and mouse with me.

Tone rummaged through the refrigerator, "Did you forget that fuck boy raped your girl or did seeing Kyrah and her son make you lose sight of all that? We're either going to put some holes in somebody or I'm going home. I told your ass never bring bullshit to the place you rest your head."

I heard Tone talking but I wasn't listening.......................

Life had just smacked me in the face. There I was in the mist of planning on killing my son's uncle, my baby mama's brother. I didn't want to make a decision that I would regret in the end but then again I couldn't let Mike get away with raping Shay and I damn sure wasn't about to let Quan's hoe ass get away with putting a couple bullets in me. Part of me wanted to run after Kyrah and be with my family but the other part of me said fuck it let's ride. I was torn in between the right thing to do and my sinister thoughts. I knew Tone was right I brought the bullshit into my home and once you bring the streets home with you it never leaves. I had never been more confused in my life.

Tone must have seen the confusion in my face," Bro I'm out. Holla at me when your head is clear and your mind is made up."

Wiping my eyes," Fa sho. Do you need a ride?"

He laughed," Man these females got you going insane. You love one, the other one got you for some bundles and claims to be having your seed while the other one waited three years to introduce you to your son. I can't deal with this shit yall nigga's need to be on Jerry Springer. I called my girl she is coming to pick me up."

We played Call of Duty until his ride came. Tone was right I did need to be on Jerry Springer and I needed a few session with Dr. Phil. My world was already fucked up enough without a son. I couldn't do shit but sit there and think. My phone was ringing off the hook. I finally took it out my pocket to see who the fuck had been calling me. There were five missed calls from Shay and each one had a voicemail to match, two from Shawn, and countless ones from my mama. I didn't feel like talking to anybody and my thoughts were already talking loud enough. I knew my mama and Shay were worried so I sent Shay a text and told her to tell my mama that everything was fine, I didn't bother hitting Shawn up.

I splashed some water on my face and headed down the basement to the studio. Music was my only way of releasing my frustrations. For years I had let music settle my anger. I hit the booth hard as hell. Before I knew it, it was three o'clock in the morning. Still not thinking clearly I went upstairs and fixed me some food. After I ate I passed out on the couch watching old episodes of the Wayans Brothers. I woke up to a loud bang at the door. I looked down at my watch and it was a little past nine.

Shay stood on the other side of the door screaming," Ant open the door.....Open the door."

Jumping up," I'm coming baby....Relax!"

I wiped the sleep from my eyes and tried to smooth the wrinkles from my clothes. When I opened the door Quan was standing there holding a gun to her back. I went to reach for my piece remembering that I had left it on the floor next to the couch. I understood at that moment why Shawn was so trigger happy and why Tone had so many guns planted around his house. I was past tired of people running up in my shit pointing guns.

Shay was in tears," I'm sor....."

Before she could finish her sentence he shouted," Bitch be quiet."

Quan pointed the gun at me," Back the fuck up nigga before I blow this bitch up to the heavens."

I put my hands up," What are you doing man, she doesn't have shit to do with this."

He aimed the gun at my head," Nigga shut the fuck up."

I regretted my decision, I should have killed the nigga last night when Tone was suited and booted to shut the nigga up for good. Shit like this happens when you leave business unfinished or when you try to consider another nigga's feelings. Kill or be killed was the number one rule of the streets.

He slammed the door behind him never taking his eyes off me and Shay," So you thought you could just fuck my chick, knock her up and get away with it."

I looked him dead in his eyes," You must not give a damn about her or yourself if you let her be out here sucking and fucking every dude that crosses her path."

I don't know what the hell was wrong with me getting cut throat with a nigga who caught me ass out. He could have easily pulled the trigger on me then Shay after some slick shit like that. I was quick tempered but now wasn't the time for that. This nigga had my life and hers in his hands. If there ever was a time for ass kissing this was it. I wasn't the type to beg for my life but I was going to do what I had to do to save Shay's.

He put the gun to Shay's head," We had a deal. Trina was supposed to get some money out of you for Mike to give to his sister and that was it. She wasn't supposed to fuck you and she damn sure wasn't supposed to get pregnant. Now the bitch is talking about she loves you and wants to be with you. I love her but just like everything else, you always get what you want."

I didn't have shit else to say. This fuck nigga was getting mad at me because he lent his chick out to one of his so called friend's to do some dirt then got mad when she got caught up in the shit. He was putting the blame on me for his stupidity. Even if it all wasn't a scam if I had known that Trina was his chick I wouldn't have even stepped to her. I wasn't the type of dude to break up happy homes even though I'm sure theirs wasn't happy. I wasn't worried about Trina, Mike or anybody else; I just didn't want Shay to pay for my mistakes. I knew I couldn't get over to the couch to reach my gun, before I even made it to the couch he would have lit my ass up. I just had to let the situation play out and hope for the best.

Shay cried out," An---t."

Quan grabbed her by the back of her neck," Bitch, you better shut the fuck up before I make you swallow these bullets."

I walked a few steps closer," Look man if you want to hurt somebody hurt me. She doesn't have shit to do with this. This is our beef not hers."

He pulled Shay closer to him," Oh this has everything to do with her. She is the only person you care about in this fucked up world. You have the only female I thought that cared about me slobbing you down and fucking you so I figure if I take this bitch out the picture you'll know exactly how I feel. The past always comes to bite you in the ass nigga remember that."

I shook my head," We were boys. If I knew that Trina was your chick I never would have stepped to her. Mike set this cat and mouse game up and it seems like we are the only people getting hurt in the situation. I talked to his sister, she never wanted any of this to happen, that nigga manipulated all of us."

He tossed Shay to the floor and pointed his 23 directly between my eyes," Nigga I don't give a fuck about Mike, his sister or this bitch on the floor. Nigga this is about me and you now. You think because Tone is your brother your untouchable."

I had a blank stare," What?"

He laughed," I don't see that nigga here now. Ever since we were in high school you and Shawn thought you could boss nigga's around, fuck our sisters and girls and never be touched. Well mutha fucka looks like I'm the big man on campus now. I respect Tone but you, I've never liked you. I hated you growing up but when Mike stepped to me with his plan I couldn't pass it up. Your friend Shawn made it all too easy with his stupidity. I had him eating from the palm of my hand and he didn't even realize it."

I was tired of playing cat and mouse," Look nigga we all did our dirt back then but we are grown ass men now. If you're going to kill me then kill me but don't stand here and stroll down memory lane about some shit that happened before we could even call ourselves men. Tone is my big brother not my body guard, he looked out for me by choice not upon request."

He put his finger on the trigger," You're talking real tough, remember bitch, I'm the one with the gun."

Shay went to get up and he let off three shots. Then he pointed the gun back at me. I could see her blood coloring my carpeting red as she gasped for air. I don't think he wanted to shoot her but it didn't matter, it was over for him. My heart felt like it was going to explode.

Tears filled my eyes," Nigga call 911."

He froze. I didn't care if he shot me but I made a mad dash for the phone. I wasn't about to sit there and watch Shay die. I would die trying to save her before I sat there and did nothing.

I grabbed the phone and dialed 911,"I need an ambulance someone has been shot."

He shot her in the shoulder and in the stomach the third bullet missed her and was stuck in the wall above her head," Baby I'm so sorry you got dragged into this. Hold on, just stay with me."

Her eyes started to roll to the back of her head. Seeing her lay helplessly on the floor made my stomach turn. A few minutes later sirens filled the morning air. Quan ran out the back door as the EMS pulled into the drive way. I watched as the EMS placed Shay carefully onto the gurney. They asked me several questions about any allergies she may have, her approximate weight, and her name. They shut the doors to the EMS and sped off down the street. I wanted to ride with her but the police were already there asking me questions about what happened. I hated the police because my track record with them wasn't all that great. As far as I was concerned they were all enemies of mine.

One female officer searched the house while her partner questioned me.

Pulling out his note pad," Sir what happened here? Do you know who did this?"

I knew who did it but I wasn't about to let him get the easy way out and just get arrested. I was going to deal with him personally. There was

85

no doubt about it Quan had the mark of the death and I was the grim reaper. Revenge is the sweetest taste and I had a sweet tooth. I'm sure Quan knew I wouldn't snitch to the police and I'm sure he knew I was coming after him. I knew Shay was going to be alright but that didn't matter the simple fact that he put a gun to her was reason enough for me to eliminate him from the world.

Clearing his throat as if I didn't hear him the first time," Sir what happened here?"

I shook my head looking at Shay's blood on my hands," My girlfriend was here by herself and I guess someone broke in thinking no one was home. I was getting out of the car and heard gunshots. When I finally got into the house I found her bleeding on the floor."

He jotted down some notes," Did you get a look at the perpetrator."

I wiped my face with my shirt," No. Look officer I really just need to get to the hospital. I'll answer any questions you have later."

The officer and his partner agreed," Here is my card. You can come down to the station tomorrow morning."

Chapter Six

I watched as the officers got in their squad car and pulled away. I was about to head to the hospital when I looked down at my clothes. My shirt and pants were stained with Shay's blood, I couldn't go anywhere looking like I had taken a blood bath. I quickly took a hot shower, got dressed and headed straight to the hospital. As I pulled out of my drive-way I saw Quan's car a few houses down. I didn't pay any mind to it because I knew that nigga was nowhere near my house. I wouldn't be surprised if he ran all the way back to his hood. He was probably at home hiding under his bed by now. I pulled off my street and saw that a few police officers were still looking for evidence and asking neighbor's questions. Rule 101 of the streets, when something jumps off, nobody knows shit they all play deaf, dumb, and blind. For once I was happy that folks didn't speak up because I wanted to handle the situation my way. When I got to the hospital I pulled up to the emergency room door and jumped out the car.

A passing security guard called out," Sorry man there is no parking here."

I shrugged my shoulders," Tow it."

I wasn't worried about a fucken ticket or my car being towed. I rushed through the swinging doors of Providence Hospital when I was stopped by the officers at the metal detector. The E.R got crazy sometimes so they searched everybody coming into the joint. I thought to myself," I don't have time for this shit." Normally the ass holes abused their power when they saw a nigga like me. Today wasn't the day for their bullshit. Luckily I didn't have anything on me but my car keys and phone, they had no choice but to let me through the metal detectors without a hassle.

Putting a smile on," Excuse me sweetheart I'm looking for a gunshot victim Le' Shay Evans?'

The nurse at the desk smiled," Are you family?"

I had to lie because I knew their policy, if you weren't a family member they couldn't disclose any information too you. I wanted to punch her in the face and look through the records but I knew she was only doing her job. I'm glad she was polite because normally there was some ghetto bird at the desk popping her gum telling me to hold on while she finished her phone conversation. I appreciated people who were polite and had people skills. I was patient with the nurse because she was showing me respect so there was no reason for me to be disrespectful or ignorant.

Nodding," Yes she is my wife."

She began typing," Mr. Evans they just took her up to surgery. It will probably be a five to six hour surgery. She was stable when they brought her in but she is in critical condition."

My face quickly twisted up and tears filled my eyes," Thank you."

She placed her hand on top of mine," We have some of the best doctors working on her, I'm sure she will be fine. Is there a number the hospital can reach you? Myself or one of the other nurses can give you a call when she is out of surgery."

I grabbed the pen and pad that was on the desk," Yes here is my cell phone number. Please call me as soon as there is any change. Thank you!"

I didn't wait for her to say anything I headed back out the double doors. I put everything in God's hands that the nurse was right. As soon as I got outside, I saw that nobody had come to tow my car and I didn't have a ticket.

The chunky security guard walked up behind me," Next time park in the structure."

I felt like turning around and bitch slapping him, but he looked out for me," Thanks man."

I jumped in the whip and peeled out of the hospital and headed straight towards Quan's house. I rummaged under the seat and found my 38. It was the only untraceable gun I had. All my other guns were legit and registered. I made sure I kept papers on my guns because possession of an unauthorized weapon was automatic time in prison. I only kept guns for protection but today all that protection shit didn't matter I was out to kill. I planned on spraying Quan's blood all over his house.

I parked around the block from Quan's house and went through the alley. The alley was full of weeds and bushes so I wasn't worried about anybody seeing me. When I reached Quan's house I could see him and Trina sitting on the bed talking. I started to turn around because my plan was only to kill him, I didn't give a fuck about her life. The devil was on my back so I remained peeking through the window. When I saw Trina leave the room I headed to the side door and saw that the kitchen window was open. I lifted the screen and reached my hand through to open the door. After several minutes of twisting and turning the door knob it finally unlocked and I crept inside the house. I pulled the screen back down and eased the door shut. To my good fortune, Trina had went into the bathroom and started the shower. I was creeping around the house like I was a little kid trying to catch Santa Clause. I can't lie, I was nervous and had doubts but all the doubt in my mind disappeared quickly when I thought about Shay fighting for her life.

I crept right up on Quan and he didn't hear shit. He was on the edge of the bed smoking a blunt and watching some bullshit show on TV. When he turned around the blunt hit the floor and he looked like he had seen a ghost.

I laughed," Nigga this is what it has to come to. You thought you were big shit huh? See Tone isn't here nigga it's just me, you, and this piece. I can fight my own battles; Tone only stepped in all the time because that is what big brothers do. I have never asked anybody to do my dirt for me, I'm fully capable of holding my own. Don't ever get it twisted nigga. "

He went to speak and I shot him twice in the chest. I stood there for a second in shock at what I had just done but I wasn't sorry for what I did. I watched as blood rushed onto his wrinkled sheets. He deserved those two bullets. If I hadn't killed him someone would have eventually. Like I said, nigga's like us have an expiration date.

I heard Trina shut the shower off," Babe?"

I walked out the back door and didn't look back. I headed back down the alley, as I was running screams rung from the house. I wiped my prints off the gun and tucked it into the back of my pants. When I got far enough away from the house I slowed down to catch my breath. After what I had just done the only person I could think about was Shay. I reached my car and drove off slowly trying to avoid any unwanted attention. I drove straight down Jefferson to Belle Isle. I sped through the park until I reached the pier. I got out the car and walked all the way to the end of the pier and just stood there. After a couple of minutes of breathing in the fresh air, I pulled the gun from my pants and tossed it into the water. I stood there and prayed. I asked God for forgiveness and direction. I prayed that Shay would make it out of surgery alive and I prayed that all this bullshit and drama was over. I asked God for the strength to help me raise my son and I asked him to wash my hands clean. For the first time in a long time I put all of my trust in the hands of God and I actually felt like I was at peace. Praying didn't minimize the million and one thoughts that I had roaming through my head but it felt good to ask for forgiveness.

As I was walking back to the car, my phone rang, it was Trina. I knew what she wanted.

I hesitated but after a few rings I answered," Hello."

Her voice was frantic," Ant....Quan is dead!"

I took a deep breath," What?"

I could hear the strain in her voice," Somebody ran up in here while I was in the shower and shot him."

I didn't feel any sympathy for her ass, she was aware of the deal with Mike. I knew she had used me so any feelings I did have for her were gone. I didn't care about her or the bastard baby she was supposedly pregnant with. I had made up my mind. I was done with her once and for all.

I cleared my throat," Damn it's all bad. Did you call the cops?"

She sniffed a few times," Yea, I just wanted someone here with me."

I looked around the park," I'm sorry Trina but I have some business that I need to handle."

Before she could say anything else I said my good-byes and hung up. Part of me felt like she really wanted me there with her and the other part of me really didn't give a fuck. I got into my car, turned up my stereo and headed back to the hospital. My stomach was in knots. If Shay died everybody would pay for what Quan had done. All types of evil thoughts roamed my head. I thought about who I would kill first. If Shay didn't make it off that operating table everybody would be having a funeral service by time the weekend rolled around. I pulled up to the hospital a quarter to six. I wasn't about to test my luck with hospital security again so I pulled around to the front entrance where the valet parking was.

The parking attendant took my keys and handed me a ticket," It will be five dollars on your way out."

She stepped into the truck and zoomed down the lot. If my truck had one scratch on it, that was her ass. I didn't drop thousands of dollars on my range for somebody else to fuck it up. Shaking the thought of my shit missing a bumper or something I preceded into the hospital entrance. I felt like I was in a bad nightmare and couldn't wake up.

The woman at the front desk shuffled through folders," May I help you?"

I smiled," Yes. I'm Le' Shay Evans husband. I was here earlier and talked to a nurse in the E.R. I wanted to know if she was out of surgery yet."

She picked up the phone," One second Mr. Evans. You can have a seat over there and a doctor will be with you in a moment."

I felt like I was walking on nails. I sat down but my nerves were so bad that I couldn't stay seated. I paced the lobby waiting for the doctor. My heart was beating so fast that it felt like I was about to have a damn heart attack. My polo shirt hugged my chest because I was sweating so much. I tugged at it to loosen it from my skin. My mind focused on negative shit I couldn't find one positive thought in my brain. I couldn't lose Shay. She was the woman I wanted to marry, the woman I wanted to have kids with. We would grow old together and live somewhere on the beach. If she died so would a piece of me.

A doctor saved me from my thoughts," Are you Mr. Evans?"

I extended my hand," Yes Dr."

He smiled," Nice to meet you Mr. Evans. I'm Doctor Graves. Your wife is settled in a room, she is still a little groggy but I will have the nurse take you up to see her in a moment. I wanted to talk to you about a few things first."

It felt like a ton of bricks had been lifted from my shoulders," Thank you so much. What is it that you wanted to talk to me about?"

His smile faded," Did you know your wife was pregnant?"

I sat down in the chairs lined against the wall," No I didn't, why?"

He placed his hand on my shoulder," From the looks of things she was about three weeks pregnant but one of the bullets was launched into the baby's skull."

I felt sick like I was about to throw up. I was happy I killed Quan because he took something away from Shay that could never be given back. He had killed an innocent life that didn't even get the chance to make it into the world. I felt tears begin to flood my eyes, I quickly wiped them away.

I lifted my head from my hands," Does she know?"

The doctor shook his head," No, I wasn't sure if either of you knew that she was pregnant. Le' Shay also lost a lot of blood so we had to give her blood transfusions. She will be down for a few weeks but she should make a full recovery. We are still running some test but there is a chance that she won't be able to have children again. We won't know for sure until we run a few test and examine the results. The important thing is that she is alive."

Although the doctor was right, I was thankful that Shay was alive but he had just dropped a heavy load right back on me. I knew I would have to be the one to tell Shay that we lost our unborn child and I wasn't prepared for that conversation. She always talked about having kids and now because of some shit I put her in the middle of, she may never be able to have kids. I was disgusted with myself. I hated the world but really the only person I could hate was myself. I was the reason for Shay's misfortune and I couldn't fix the problem. There are no words to say to a person to relieve them of their pain. Pain makes a home where it isn't welcome and doesn't leave until its good and ready.

The doctor signaled for one of the passing nurses to direct me to Shay's room.

I extended my hand," Thanks again Doc."

He gripped my hand firmly," Your welcome. I will come check on Le' Shay during my rounds."

I walked along side the nurse. We took the elevator up to the 10th floor. Every step we took made my stomach groan louder. I was nervous like a child on their first day of school. My forehead was beaded with sweat and my hands were clammy. We walked down to the end of the hallway to the last room on the left. I thought if I walked slowly that it would give me time to think of what to say.

She opened the door," Here we are room 223."

I smiled," Thanks."

I stood outside the door for a few seconds working up the courage to go in. I tried to think about what I was going to say before I was going to say it but it didn't matter what I said nothing would make things right. I walked through the threshold and glanced around the room. There were several machines but there she was with a smile on her face as if nothing was wrong. I admired Shay for still being able to smile after all she had been though.

Her voice was raspy," Hey baby!"

I fought back the tears I felt coming," Hey solider!"

We both giggled.

I pulled the chair from across the room and sat it next to her bed. We just sat there holding hands. In a way, I guess we both knew what was going on. I hated seeing her in pain. I wish I could have taken the bullets for her. She looked a little pale but that was to be expected since she had loss so much blood. I couldn't find my words, I just sat there holding her hand. I held onto to her palm tightly as if she was keeping me alive. When she fell asleep I closed my eyes and asked God to make the pain go away. I prayed aloud as I clinched her hand," God I know I haven't always sought your help much over the years but I'm begging you to help me make this right. I know I have sinned but this isn't about me this is about Shay. Please give her the strength to face her darkest hours, please heal her body and mind...Amen."

I never really prayed so I wasn't sure if I was doing it right but as long as God could hear me I guess there was no right or wrong way to do it. I never expected God to look out for me but I was hoping that he could

watch over Shay.

Chapter Seven

The nurse knocked on the door," I'm sorry honey but visiting hours are ending or were you planning on staying the night?"

I gently slid my hand from Shays," Yes, I'm going to stay."

She smiled," Alright, I just need you to go down to the front desk and get an overnight pass. I will let the nurse down there know your coming."

I looked back at Shay to make sure she was still sleeping," Ok, no problem. Thanks!"

I headed out the door behind her.

As I walked down the hall she ran after me," I wasn't trying to listen in on what you were saying but I'm sure God has forgiven you and I'm sure he will answer your prayers."

Any other time I probably would have snapped at the fact that someone was ear hustling but she was only trying to help. It was always strange to me how some of the kindest words came from a stranger's mouth. I always felt like God was never there but I was beginning to realize that you have to call upon him for blessings to be answered, you can't expect things to change overnight. The nurse extended her arms and flashed me a warm smile.

I embraced her," Thank you, I needed to hear that!"

She whispered," Everything happens for a reason and sometimes we don't understand these reasons but one day everything will make sense."

I smiled, I needed to hear some encouraging words because at the moment it felt like my life was falling apart. I thanked her again and walked towards the elevator. When I got to the first floor the nurse already had my overnight pass ready. I got back to the room and Shay was still sound asleep so I stepped into the hallway to make a few phone calls. I had to call my mama because she had already called me several times and I had to holla at Tone and Shawn to see what was going on. I knew they probably had heard about Quan but I wanted to know exactly what they had heard.

When I called my mama she picked up the phone on the first ring," Boy what in the world is going on? I've called you more than enough times. Are your ears broken, you can't hear your phone ringing? Are you ok? Where is Shay, some man picked her up and she ran out of here so quick, I didn't know what was going on. Are you in trouble? Is Shay in trouble, where is your brother?"

She didn't take a breath," Boy I know you hear me talking to you."

I laughed," Ma, you haven't given me a chance to say anything."

She snarled," Don't get smart with me, your not too old for me to whoop you."

We both laughed.

Clearing my throat," I'm okay ma. Shay got shot today but she is going to be okay. I'd rather talk to you face to face and tell you everything."

I could hear her voice softening," Oh my lord. I knew something was suspicious the way she darted out of here. I'm glad that she is ok, I'm going to pray for you both."

I smiled, "Thanks mama! I will be by to see you tomorrow."

She agreed," Ok baby give Shay my love."

Even though we didn't say too much, hearing her voice made me feel a lot better. I called Tone but he didn't answer, he probably was with one of his freaks. When I called Shawn he picked up the phone talking ten miles per minute just like my mama.

I leaned against the wall," Slow down. What's the word nigga?"

I could tell he was smoking," Shit nigga. You know somebody ran in Quan's crib and popped that nigga."

I smirked," Yeah I heard."

I planned on telling Shawn that it was me who killed Quan but not over the phone. I learned a lot from my older brother and one thing you never did was talk about business or the dirt you've done over the phone, somebody is always listening.

We bullshitted for a minute before I got back to inquiring about the streets," So, you heard anything about Mike."

He sniffed," Nope the streets been quiet since Quan got bagged."

I smiled to myself," Word. Kyrah came to see me and we talked about some shit."

His voiced heightened," Hell yeah. Shit nigga what happened?"

I laughed," Nothing nigga we just talked. She told me she wanted all this beef shit to end."

Coughing," Shit don't we all but it isn't that easy, nigga's have to die before they see peace. Did you tell Shay that you saw her?"

I hesitated," I haven't gotten the chance to tell her yet."

Rummaging in the background," Oh I feel you, she might kick yo ass."

We both laughed," Clown.......Look we need to meet up tomorrow man on some real shit."

Seriousness took over his voice," Iight man, just hit me up."

We had a few more words then I hung up the phone. I was debating whether or not I should have told Shawn about Shay being shot but for the time being I would just keep it to myself. For now the only person who knew was my mama and I planned to keep it that way until morning. I knew Shawn knew something was up but now wasn't the time to get into all that, I turned my phone off and went back into the room. I sat in the chair next to Shay's bed watching her sleep, she looked so peaceful. I planned on telling her everything in the morning. She deserved to know what was going on and I needed to man up and tell her. I drowned myself with thoughts until I drifted off to sleep, tomorrow would be a new day.

When I woke up the next morning it was eight thirty, my back and neck hurt like hell, I felt like someone had beaten the shit out of me. Sleeping in the hospital chair was the most uncomfortable night of sleep I ever had, it was worse than sleeping on a hardwood floor. I looked over and Shay was scrolling through the channels. Although she was tied to machines and her hair was messy, she still looked beautiful. I watched as she became frustrated with the hospitals channel selection, it was either the news or a crappy movie.

She smiled," Good morning!"

It amazed me how warm she was with me. Most females would have been ready to bite my head off or kill me if it was my fault that they had gotten shot. I could see the pain in her eyes even though she smiled to try and cover it up. Shay has always been a strong person but with everything that was going on I could see that is was taking a toll on her. I wish I could rewind the hands of time and change how things turned out but I knew that wasn't possible.

I leaned over and kissed her forehead," Good morning beautiful! How are you feeling?"

She laughed," Like I've been shot!"

I smiled," Okay smart ass!"

We sat there talking for an hour before I worked up enough courage to tell her everything that was on my chest. I started with the fact that I had a son. I told her all about Kyrah and our three year old son that I had just met the day before. I paused behind every sentence in case there was something she wanted to say. She sat there listening to every word I said never taking her eyes off of me. I continued on with telling her why Quan damn near killed me and her along with the scheme involving Mike and Trina. I wanted to tell her that I had killed Quan but I knew that was one secret I couldn't share. Even though she knew most of my secrets I would never burden her with one about murder, certain things eat at a person conscious even if they aren't the ones who did the actual crime.

She pulled me close to her breast," Baby, I can't hold your mistakes against you. We all have secrets and we all have made mistakes. I will always be here for you whether we are together or friends, you will always hold a special place in my heart that nobody else will ever be able to fill."

I smiled," I'm not finished......PAUSING.....Did you know you were pregnant?"

She nodded," Yes, I was waiting for the right time to tell you."

I looked down at the floor. Damn, her knowing that she was pregnant was going to make it even harder for me to tell her that there was no longer a baby. My mistakes had caused her and our unborn child to be the ones to suffer but I had to tell her one way or another. I took a deep breath in order to find my words. I tried to find the perfect words but there were no perfect words to say what I had to say. No matter what way I put it or what words I said, it was going to crush her. I wasn't sure if Shay could even handle anymore bad news but I swallowed what pride I had left and broke the bad news to her.

She grabbed my face and looked me in my eyes," What is wrong? Is there something wrong with the baby?"

I grabbed her hand," You lost the baby. The bullet was lodge in the baby's head. There was nothing the doctors could do."

Tears filled her bright brown eyes," I---iiii just want to be alone."

I pressed my hand across her cheek," Are you sure?"

She closed her eyes to stop the flow of salty tears," Yes."

I stood up and straightened out my clothes," Okay baby. I'll be back a little later."

She just kept her eyes closed and turned her back to me. I felt like I was less than a man, I was disgusted with myself. I just wanted to hold her and tell her that I loved her but I couldn't. I knew she resented me, I was the reason our baby was dead. I couldn't change what was done but even if there was some way to fix it, we would never be the same again. I respected her wishes and headed out the door trying to console my pain and anger. We both needed some time to ourselves just to think and to get our emotions under control. I took the elevator down to the lobby and hunted down the valet attendant, I dug through my pockets to find my parking stub. I handed the stub to the valet and he shot off into the morning air, I stood there embracing the cool breeze against my skin. I felt like breaking down and crying but I held myself together, crying wasn't going to solve my problems. Everything that was happening was really weighing me down but I had to stay strong, there was no time for tears, the smell of revenge lingered in my nostrils.

 The valet returned with my truck and handed me the keys," That will be five dollars."

 I walked around the car to check for any damage then pulled out my wallet and gave him twenty dollars," Keep the change."

 I pulled out of the hospital driveway and went straight home. I needed a shower before I went to see my mama. I pulled in my drive way finding police tape everywhere. My front yard looked like a big murder investigation on display for the whole neighborhood to see. I opened the door and the first thing I saw was the blood stain left from Shay, I still couldn't believe that shit happened. I wasn't sure if the cops were finished looking through my place but I wasn't about to leave a big ass blood stain in the middle of my carpet. I went into the kitchen and searched for any cleaning supplies I had. It took forever for me to lift the large stain from the carpet. I had gotten most of it up but I still needed to have the carpet cleaned inorder to fully remove the blood, in the meantime I just placed a rug on top of it because I couldn't have my shit looking raggedy. It's funny how I was so worried about bloody carpet when I was in the middle of shit storm. I put the cleaning supplies back under the sink and headed to my room. I shifted through my closet and pulled out some jeans, a white-t, grabbed a pair of Jordan's and my black fitted Detroit hat. When I stepped into the bathroom I almost bust my ass on a towel that was in the middle of the floor. I sat on the edge of the shower until the water was hot, the bathroom was layered with a thin puff of white steam. I scrubbed my body as if I could scrub my problems away, the warm water felt good dripping down my aching body. As I was getting dressed I forgot that I turned my phone off so I turned it on to check my messages. I had three voicemails and they all were from Trina begging me to come over.

I dialed her number and waited for her to pick up, after a couple of rings her voice echoed through the phone. We talked for a minute then she asked me to come over. I was expecting her to ask me, so I agreed. I needed to cut it off with her once and for all, her game was spent and it was about time she got wind of that shit. I had too much on my plate already, I wasn't about to deal with her shit another minute. I locked up my crib and headed down the lodge to her house. When I got there the door was already open so I walked in. Her house smelled like fresh cinnamon rolls making my empty stomach fall in love with the aroma. Looking around her spacious house I knew that her tricking days paid off because her house was laid. She had brand new furniture and big ass TV's. Her house looked like something you saw on MTV Cribs or the Fabulous Life of, I was very impressed.

She greeted me with a hug," I'm so glad to see you. I missed you."

Pushing her away," Let's get this over with. Your nigga is dead and I know what you were doing for Mike. There is no longer any reason for us to be speaking. When you see me on the street don't even look at me. We're done. Don't come by my crib, don't call me, don't call Shawn looking for me, and don't post up outside the studio. Be a mere figment of my imagination."

Her attitude changed quick as hell," Nigga fuck you. Everybody thinks I'm just some hoe with no feelings, but I thought you were different. I told that nigga that I was out of his twisted game, I was at Quan's house this morning breaking things off with him but your too busy sniffing up your so called best-friends ass that you wouldn't know that. I should have known you would pick that bitch over me. The little prissy bitches always get the nigga that they want."

I snapped," Bitch don't give me that. You ain't shit but a stripper who gets any nigga's dick wet who is willing to break bread on your ass. You had me caught up for a minute and I tried to be on your side when nigga's called you out but now I see for myself you ain't shit but a microwave bitch, a fucken hot n ready. You play too many games to keep a man, shit you had me but you were just scheming on me so blame yourself. "

She picked up a vase and tossed it at me. I tried to dunk but that shit happened so fast it bust me upside the head. I felt a drop of blood hit my arm as it trickled down the side of my face. My mama taught me to never lay my hands on a woman but that bitch had already pushed too many of my buttons. I felt like I was about to bust out of my clothes like the hulk and molly wop her ass to the floor. Women always talk about men hitting them but they provoke the shit. I hadn't put my hands on her or thrown shit at her but she had to be childlike and prove why most men don't like black women. She did me dirty and played with my emotions but still expected me to be with her. After all this was over, a nigga was going to need to see a shrink and get a prescription for some anxiety pills.

I pushed her against the wall," Don't call me anymore, bitch were done."

She kneed me in the balls," Get the fuck out."

My anger got the best of me, before I knew it I had her choked up against the wall. She was scratching at my arm; I could feel her nails digging into my skin. I wanted to snap her neck like a chicken but I let her go and walked out the door. I managed to let her get inside my head which caused me to snap. I knew if my mama had seen what I had done she would have been so ashamed. I had to get out of there before things got any worse, I didn't want two murders on my hands.

She ran up behind me," Nigga fuck you. I hope all yall nigga's rot in hell."

I laughed," Trick if we do we will surely see you there as well."

She stood at the door glaring at me as if she was placing a curse on my life. I didn't waste any more time arguing with her, the neighbors stood around whispering and pointing. I sped off down the street and hit the brakes just in time to avoid hitting a car pulling out of their drive-way. I turned on some jazz to sooth my nerves. I drove to my mama's house but the whole time I drove the only thing I could think about was turning around and beating the shit out of Trina. My forehead had a big ass gash across it and my arms were all scratched up and bloody. I stopped at a gas station to clean myself up. Staring in the mirror I wondered who the fuck I had become. Was I a killer? Was the shit I did justified? Was I getting what I deserved? Who was the person looking back at me? I didn't recognize the man looking back at me.

A woman was beating on the door," Aye man can you hurry up, my daughter has to pee."

I opened the door," Damn, ease up lady."

She brushed passed me," Asshole."

I ignored her because the way I was feeling I could have clocked her upside the head. I got in my truck and pulled out the gas station. I drove the rest of the way to my mama's house in silence. When I pulled up the front door was open I knew she had been waiting for me. I cut the engine off and took a deep breath before I got out of the car. I walked up the stairs to the house and it felt like I was walking to the electric chair. I already knew my mama was about to grill me to the third degree. If nobody else set my ass straight she would. As soon as I opened the door she slapped me in the back of my head. My mama was 5"8 and about 160 lbs but when she hit you, you would have thought "The Rock" bitch slapped you with a phone book. The back of my neck was stinging, I had to remind myself that she was my mother because I was tempted to smack her back.

I grabbed my head," Damn ma, what was that for?"

She shook her head," For being a hard headed fool and what in the world happened to your head? You look terrible."

I lied," Nothing I bumped it on the car door."

Walking towards the kitchen," Sure you did and I guess a kitten scratched your arms up. You hungry?"

Still holding my head," No, I'm good."

I was hungry as hell but I didn't want to put her through the trouble of fixing me something. I wanted to run and hide in the closest like I did as a kid.

She pulled out a chair," You know Ms. Tyler's boy was murdered yesterday, do you know anything about that?"

Ms. Tyler was Quan's mama. I couldn't just be like yeah mama I know, I'm the one who did it. I felt bad for Ms. Tyler because I knew she was hurting right now. Her youngest son Richard had been killed a few years back in a car accident, Quan was all she had. I would pay my respects to her but I still didn't regret my decision. I was sorry that she had to be hurt in the process but that was life, shit bad things happen to good people like her all of the time.

I sat down," Damn fa real."

She nodded," Yes and boy I already told you if you don't stop talking to me like I'm one of your little friends I'm going to slap the taste out your mouth."

I laughed," My bad mama I forget sometimes."

She sipped her coffee," Mm Hmm I'm sure you do. So what is this business about Shay and when were you going to tell me you had a son?"

I instantly knew she had been talking to Tone. We were two grown ass men but we always told our mama everything, like when we were kids. I laughed to myself remembering the time I told her that I had saw Tone smoking weed in the backyard and a few months later our youngest sister caught both of use smoking after school and we both got our asses smacked up. It was always a contest between Tone and me but our sisters

117

took that shit to a whole new level, they use to get us in trouble every other day. Shaking my head, I remembered the question my mother had just asked me.

I rubbed my eyes," Somebody came in my house while she was there and shot her and yes mama Kyrah showed up with my son. His name is Christopher and he is three years old. He looks just like me when I was a kid."

I could hear the excitement in my own voice when I was telling her about Chris. It felt good to know that I had a son and it felt even better for my mother to know that she had a grandson. I knew that even if something happened to me my mama would always have a piece of me left behind. I wasn't going to tell her that the person who ran up in my crib was Quan because then she would have asked me was I the one who killed him or did I pay someone to kill him. The less my mother knew about what was going on between Mike, Trina, Quan and I, the better. Silence moved through the air. I already knew my mama was disappointed in me and I was disappointed in myself for lying to her. I wanted to tell my mama so badly what was going on but I couldn't. I couldn't tell my mother that I had become a killer. I already knew that I had brought a lot of shame to myself and I wasn't about to tally up killing someone to the list of things I shared with her.

She cleared her throat," I can't believe my baby has a baby. Now what about this Trina girl, did you find out if the baby was yours?"

Rearranging stuff on the table," No it's not my baby and I'm done with her anyway."

She placed her hand on top of mine," Son I taught you everything I could. I raised you the best way I knew how but I can't teach you how to be a man it's one of those things that you learn along the way. I'm sorry your father decided to walk out on us but I tried to raise all you kids to be humble and respectful. You can't keep treating women like old toys, once you are tired of playing with them you toss them to the side and move onto the next one. I really hope you've learned a lesson from all of this. You're my baby and I will love you regardless of what you do but sooner or later you have to stop and look at your actions and learn from your mistakes."

Flashing a smile," Mama you did a great job raising all of us. Somewhere down the line I just got caught up with wanting to be popular that I forgot who I was. I'm working on becoming the man I know you raised me to be. I know I have to do right by Kyrah for the sake of our child and I plan on doing right by Shay. I've been a fool for awhile but recently I've become aware of the results of my actions."

She hugged me," I hope so son. I know you have a big heart and I know you're a good man. You just have to search inside yourself to find the man who is trying to burst out. I would love to keep up this talk but I have to head down to a meeting at the youth center."

My mother was the founder of a non-profit youth center. She had opened the youth center almost five years ago for children five to nineteen. She tried to help anyone she could whether it was helping them find a job, stay out of prison, or get their G.E.D. Although my mother held a PhD in education she dedicated all of her time to running the youth center. If she wasn't helping a child she was in a meeting trying to improve the youth program. The city needed more people like my mother, people willing to help who weren't worried about how much money they were going to get paid. She did everything in her power to keep young kids off the streets, and in school. I couldn't count how many people she helped graduate from high school and get into college over the years.

I stood up," Yea I have to go see Tone any way."

She walked over to the sink," Remind that knuckle head to call me."

I waited for my mother to grab her purse and we walked out together. I kissed her on the cheek and walked down the driveway to my truck. As I pulled into the street I waved good-bye and proceeded down the block. I decided to take the street to Tone's house instead of the freeway. I was stopped at a light when I saw police lights flashing in my rearview mirror, which made me regret my decision about not taking the freeway. I pulled over to the side of the road. A million things rushed through my head. I had a gun in the car but it was legit. I wasn't sure what the fuck was going on. I thought maybe it was just some asshole cops fucking with me because I was a young black man driving around in an expensive car. I had been pulled over numerous times by police officers because they thought my car was stolen, so it wasn't anything new to me.

Chapter Eight

I rummaged through my glove compartment box and had my license and registration ready to hand the officers, I turned off the engine to my truck and place my hands on the steering wheel. I knew their whole little routine, police always pulled you over just to fuck with a nigga.

The officer and his partner stepped out the car with their guns pointed," Throw the keys to the vehicle on the ground and place your hands out of the window."

I did what they said because one wrong move and I knew they would have ten bullets in my ass before they stopped to see if I had a weapon. Police were already crazy but Detroit cops were a different kind of crazy. They would beat your ass even after you surrendered then they would plant some shit on you to cover their tracks and make their actions seem justified. I hated the police but I knew not to test them. I had a gut feeling that something crazy was about to happen but I kept my cool.

The officers continued to ease their way up to the car," Step out of the car and put your hands behind your head."

I slowly opened the door and put my hands by behind my head, as they requested.

The officers rushed me," Are you Anthony King?"

I nodded," Yes, what seems to be the problem officers?"

One officer forcefully placed me in hand cuffs and pushed me into the back of the police car while the other searched through my truck. The officer's spent several minutes searching through my shit throwing papers and C.D's around. I didn't know what they were expecting to find or why they even stopped me. One officer was a husky ass nigga, who needed to lay off the donuts. He was an older guy with salt and pepper hair and stood about six feet. The other officer was a pretty boy, he was clean cut and looked cut up but he probably only stood about five foot five. I could tell he had the Napoleon complex. I sat in the back of the car waiting for them to come back and say I was going down to the station. They didn't tell me why I was in hand cuffs and they were searching through my shit without a warrant or my consent so they really didn't have a case even if they did arrest me for the gun. I had been to court several times so I knew my rights and I knew the conditions in which an officer could search my property. I wasn't worried the gun was legit and there wasn't anything else in my truck, they wouldn't be able to hold a nigga too long. Their probable cause was probably pure speculation. After about ten minutes of destroying my shit the pretty boy got on a radio and called a tow truck.

I leaned forward," Aye man why am I in cuffs?"

He laughed," For slapping up my cousin Trina, nigga.'

I was fucked, I didn't know what these two dirty ass cops were about to do to me. I knew one thing, once I was out the damn cuffs God himself wouldn't be able to stop me from getting Trina's ass. I sat in the back of the police car just watching as those two mutha fuck's destroyed my truck. The older officer thought it would be funny to piss on my interior while the other dented the doors with his Billy Stick. When the tow truck arrived they handed him the keys, shared a few words then got into the police car and the three of us pulled away.

The pretty boy laughed," So little nigga you've been knocking my cousin around? Don't think I didn't find that gun in your car and there is a nice amount of dope in the evidence room with your name on it."

I didn't say shit, fury burned through my eyes. The two officers were just poking fun at me telling me all the shit that they could do to me. The older officer took it a little too far when he painted a mental picture of me being another nigga's bitch. It took every bone in my body for me to keep my mouth shut. The officers eventually shut up and we rode the rest of the way to the police station in silence. When we reached the station I demanded to get my phone call. I wasn't about to spend anytime in jail for that bitch. Shit, from the looks of things it looked like she had kicked my ass regardless of the fact that I choked her up.

A female cop took my prints and photo then walked me over to a phone. She removed my hand cuffs," Make it quick."

I dialed Tone's number in six seconds flat when he picked up the phone I didn't even wait for him to say hello," Aye bro I just got arrested on some bullshit I need you to call Jim and bring a couple of stacks to the 36th district precinct I'm good for it when I get out."

Tone didn't ask any questions," I got you bro."

I hung up the phone and the female officer didn't hesitate to throw the cuffs back on me and put me in a holding cell. The only thing I could think about was kicking Trina's front teeth out and her bitch ass cousins. The cell was small as hell and smelled like piss there were a couple of other nigga's in there. I wasn't worried about them because they all looked like little chicken shit ass nigga's who probably just had been in holding for some bullshit possession charges or some other petty shit. I looked over at the clock on the wall it felt like days had passed. After about two hour's I was growing impatient. Among several other reasons for wanting to break loose, I needed to get back to the hospital and check on Shay. Thinking of her eased my mind and it put me in a better place.

An officer walked up to the cell," King, your lawyer is here."

I stood up and waited for the bars to open. I knew I could count on Tone. I requested Jim Matthews because he won damn near every case he was given. The nigga was expensive but well worth it, he had gotten Tone off a twenty year bid because of evidence tampering and fucked around and got him off another bid because of the double jeopardy law. Damn near every dope man, killer, and two strike nigga requested him as their attorney if they had the money to pay up. I had never been so glad to see a white man in my life, I could have kissed his feet I was so damn happy. The officer led us down a long dim hallway to an interrogation room. The room was dim and only had a few chairs, a table, and a water dispenser.

Shaking his hand," Thanks for coming on such short notice Jim."

He opened his brief case," No problem, you know your brother and I go way back."

The officers sat across the table giving me all kinds of sideways looks. I didn't pay them any mind, I knew that anything they tried to charge me with wouldn't stick. I didn't have any doubts about hiring Jim as my lawyer. I had my arms crossed waiting for the cards to unfold.

Jim placed a note pad and pen on the table," So gentlemen what are the charges that my client was arrested on."

The fat officer sat there silently with his arms folded, I could tell that he was nervous. Police officers agreed to whatever their partners wanted to do and he had agreed to some shit that he was about to regret. I didn't give a shit what happened to them as far as their jobs but I knew somebody would be paying for the damages to my truck. That fat fucker was on an ego trip when he pissed in my shit, so I defiantly had no remorse for him. I knew that Jim was about to make them regret ever fucking with me.

Clearing his throat," Gentlemen do either of you have a wife and kids?"

The pretty boy laughed," I don't think that is any of your business white boy."

Jim smiled," You see I think it is. I'm sure you know what falsifying evidence means. I'm sure you're familiar with what happens to dirty cops who get sent to prison. I'm sure you like your jobs and the little bit of power that you have obtained through your positions and I'm pretty sure both of you officers would like to keep your jobs considering the state in which our economy is in."

I could see the sweat beads forming on their foreheads. Jim wasn't a joke. He could make a grown ass man cry like a thirteen year old girl. I remember he fought one of my home boy's cases and the D.A was at a loss for words. Regardless of what the two shit heads could pull out of their ass it was no match for Jim's quick witted tongue. I just sat back and enjoyed the show.

Jim looked at me," Anthony what were the charges they supposedly arrested you on?"

I shrugged my shoulders," The only thing I remember pretty boy over there saying was "so little nigga you think you can knock my cousin around." I wasn't read my rights. I didn't give them consent to search my car, they didn't present me with a warrant and they fucked up my truck and old dough boy over there peed on my interior."

The fat cop looked like he had shit himself. I sat there with a big ass grin on my face. My boy Jim was about to hand them their dicks on a golden platter. Shit I even thought about fucking around and suing their asses, I'm sure fat boy would enjoy being someone's bitch. It was so quiet in the room you could hear a pen drop. The look on pretty boys face was definitely a Kodak moment. I didn't have to say anything else because Jim was more than handling it.

Jim stacked his papers," So you didn't read my client his rights, you searched his property without probable cause, his permission or a warrant, you destroyed his personal property, placed threats on him, brought family matters into his arrest, and let's not forget the indecent exposure charge that your facing for urinating in his vehicle as well as racial slurs....Did I leave anything out gentlemen?"

The two officers blankly stared at one another then the fat boy spoke," Look we can settle this right now. All the charges will be dropped and the four of us can shake hands and walk out of here like this never happened."

Jim laughed," So you two think this can just disappear? That's what is wrong with the legal system; fine gentlemen such as you think everything can just be swept under the rug. I won't settle for a hand shake and a pat on my clients back. You officers were out of line and I will be drawing up the papers to bring a lawsuit against the both of you and this precinct. The charges against Mr. King will be dismissed because they aren't legit charges in the first place and I will see to it that he doesn't pay a dime for bail."

I could tell that the words coming from Jim's mouth had thrown the two officers off of their pedestal. The police always thought they ruled the world because they had a badge and a gun, but without the badge they were just niggas with guns. Most of the time they got away with things such as this but they couldn't throw the sheet over Jim's eyes. I loved the way Jim talked to people it was like he gave them a compliment in the same breath that he insulted them. Jim was an arrogant lawyer but he had every right to be, he had me shaking in my Jordan's when I was the innocent one. I didn't have any worries because I already knew I was a free man. The officers didn't play it smart. They put together a half ass plan that blew up in their faces. I guess they figured I didn't have such a witty lawyer, or they thought I was going to bend under pressure. Either way, it didn't matter to me, their fuck up was about to rain down on their whole precinct and probably cost them their jobs and maybe even result to them doing a little time in the pen.

Jim gathered his papers and stacked them on top of his brief case," I didn't get your names."

The officers hung their heads low like two children who had just gotten in trouble by their mother. I just sat back and watched Jim soak their sorry ass's up like gravy on biscuit.

The large officer blurted," Alvin Moss."

The pretty boy looked at me," David Walker."

Jim wrote their names on a blank piece of paper," Well Mr. Moss and Mr. Walker you will be hearing from me very soon. I strongly suggest that my client be released within the next hour."

Officer Moss nodded," He will be released as soon as I draw up the papers."

Jim neatly placed everything back into his briefcase," I would appreciate it if you did it in a timely and orderly fashion, enough of Mr. Kings time has been wasted and officers if I were you I would get a lawyer."

Walker slammed his chair on the floor," This isn't over Anthony. I'll catch up with you on the street."

I nodded," Is that a threat."

He looked at me and walked out of the interrogation room without saying another word. Moss shook his head and followed behind Walker. I knew he would probably come after me in the streets but there was no way he would try to arrest me again. I figured Trina sent him after me because she was all shook up. Eventually I would have to deal with both of them but for now I just wanted to get out of the police station without further problems.

Jim patted me on the back," Everything here is under control. If you want me to follow through with the lawsuit let me know, I don't need an answer now just think about it. I will have a car delivered to you from the dealership until we can get your truck repaired and cleaned. I will stay and assure that you are released."

Rubbing the scratches on my arms," Thanks Jim! I just want the damages for my truck to be paid, I don't care what happens to those cops."

Jim nodded," I assure you that your truck will be restored to its original state. In my professional opinion I would draw up a law suit against the department and Officer Walker, he seems to be the master mind behind the arrest."

It was something to think about especially since it probably wasn't the end of the situation. Jim was right but at the same time I had enough problems without being dragged in and out of court. I wanted Walker and Moss to pay for their premature actions but I wasn't sure if a lawsuit was the pay back I was looking for. In time I would figure out what to do about them but for the moment I just wanted to be at the hospital with Shay. Almost thirty minutes had passed before officer Moss returned and told me that I was free to go. I felt bad for Moss because he had gotten placed into some deep shit because of his partner but my mindset quickly changed when the image of him pissing in my truck reappeared. He had a brain and he had a choice, fuck both of their crooked asses.

Jim made a few phone calls and had a 2010 Cadillac delivered to the precinct.

He laughed," I know this isn't a Range Rover but it will hold you over until we can get everything sorted out. I'll be in touch but if you have any questions or concerns in the mean time feel free to call my office and my cell phone number is on the back of my card."

Laughing," Naw this is cool Jim. Thanks again man."

Closing the trunk to his Bentley," No problem Anthony."

I spotted Tone parked on the corner so I flagged him down. He was nervous about being around the police too long so he kept his distance. I didn't blame him, especially after what just happened to me. I respect children more than I respected police officers. I think the thing that they often forgot was they are just regular people with uniforms and a little power.

Rolling down his window," Follow me to my crib."

I agreed. We took side streets to his house to avoid the heavy traffic due to construction. For some reason every summer there was construction on damn near all the main roads of the city. Taking the side streets seem to take longer due to the stop signs but it was less time consuming than the stop and go traffic near the construction. When we pulled up to his house he hoped out his car and got into the Cadillac with me.

Checking out the car," Did Jim look out for you?"

I nodded," Yeah, of course."

He fiddled with the C.D player," Good. So what are you going to do?"

I leaned my chair back," About what?"

He laughed," Don't play dumb. You know what I'm talking about Mike, Trina, and these bitch ass cops."

Scratching my chin," I don't know bro. I'm just worried about Shay. I'll worry about the rest of this mess when the time comes."

Tone nodded," I feel you."

We sat and talked for a minute laughing at the cops and their idiotic actions. I was just glad things hadn't gotten any worse. Those cops could have easily just put a bullet in me and said I shot at them first. I was

thankful that they had pulled that little scheme because I could be in the

morgue right now. I knew a few people that had gotten killed by some

scandalous cops. I would have to watch my back from now on because I

knew Officer Walker was serious, that wouldn't be the last time I saw

him. I started to apologize to Trina in hopes that maybe she could get him

to lay off but I wasn't about to give her the satisfaction. Like everything

else I would cross that bridge when the time came.

Tone opened the car door," light bro I'm out."

I watched as he walked into his crib as I drove off. I turned on the

radio and made my way to the freeway. I would try my hand at getting

Shay to at least look at me again. There wasn't anything I could do to

make things right between me and her I just had to be there in case she

needed me. I pulled out my phone and called Kyrah. It was about time that

I made things right between us. She didn't answer so I left her a message.

I wanted to meet up with her so we could talk. I put my phone in my

pocket and turned up the radio, Young Jeezy's song lose my mind was on.

I knew how he felt because I was two seconds away from losing my mind.

With everything that was going on I'm surprised I hadn't lost it already. I just let the music flow through my mind hoping that it would calm me.

Chapter Nine

When I pulled up to the hospital it was five o'clock. I only had a few dollars on me so I pulled into the area where parking was free and walked around to the hospitals main entrance. I didn't stop at the front desk because I already knew what room Shay was in. My head was pounding and my mouth was dry, my nerves were fired up. When I got to the fifth floor my heart was racing, I wasn't ready for what might happen. I don't think I could take it if Shay no longer wanted me in her life. I honestly loved her and I didn't want to lose her. I walked slowly down the long hallway until I reached her room. Taking a deep breath I knocked on the door.

She called out," Who is it?"

I gently announced myself," Anthony."

Clearing her throat," Come in."

I slowly pushed the door open and forced myself to put one foot in front of the other. I entered the room and closed the door behind me. This was the moment of truth. She would either forgive me for the pain I had caused her or she would rip me a new asshole then send me on my way like a puppy with its tail between its legs. I held my head up and sucked any ounce of manhood I had left and set on the bed next to her. I could feel a knot in my stomach from being so nervous.

She placed her arm around me," We will move forward from this."

I let out a deep sigh," You don't know how happy I am to hear that. This….."

She put her finger over my lip," Shhh... It's okay."

She removed her finger and gently kissed me. When our lips met it was like all my problems disappeared. For that moment it was just me and her. Everything that was on my mind, disappeared for those few seconds. Our embrace let me know that she had forgiven me. I wrapped my arms around her small frame and enjoyed the warmth from her body. It didn't matter what we were doing or where we were it seemed like she always made everything okay. I wanted to confess all my sins to her and tell her about the fight I had with Trina but I was a coward. I was afraid that after everything was said and done she wouldn't be able to forgive me. I had so many people's blood on my hands, I would have to take what I had done to the grave. At that moment I decided to keep what happened at Quan's house to myself, it would just have to be one secret that I never told.

Dr. Graves entered the room," How is my favorite patient?"

Shay looked at me," I'm good Dr. Graves."

He smiled," That is wonderful. I have the test results there is no permanent damage. I just recommend that you wait at least two months before trying to have another child to assure that everything is healed properly. I would like to keep you for a few more days just to make sure that the stitches are holding up and to get your iron levels back up."

Shay let out a sigh of relief," Thank you so much Dr.!"

I smiled," Yes, thank you!"

Dr. Graves nodded," No problem and Anthony you take good care of our patient."

I laughed,' I assure you that I will."

Dr. Graves checked Shay's blood pressure and her IV," I'll have the nurse bring you some pain medicine. I will be back tomorrow to check on you, have a good day!"

We thanked the doctor and then we quickly settled back into each other's arms. Even though our baby had been killed, Shay still had the opportunity to have children in the future. I felt at ease knowing that she was going to be alright. With everything going on her health was my main concern.

Shay rested her head on my shoulder," Anthony I really love you and want to build a life with you but I refuse to be with you if you're going to live your life revolved around the streets. Your music career has brought you success so there is no need for you to ruin it with silly feuds. I'm willing to leave the past behind us if you can promise me that you will do the same, otherwise this relationship will not work. I couldn't bear to see anything happen to you, I would lose my mind."

It took me a few moments to find my words. I wanted to promise her that she was my priority and that I would leave the whole Mike and Trina situation alone. I wasn't sure if I could do that so I wasn't sure if I could promise her anything, Mike and Trina hurt my pride. They both had knocked me off my square and I hated that shit. Shay was more important than my pride so I would be a fool not to promise her that I would let the past be the past. My music was on the right track and I was well taken care of, she was right getting involved with all the drama was foolish on my behalf. I did have a son and I needed to be a humble man for his sake. I needed to let go of all the bullshit for my mother, I was slowly killing her with lies. So many people were being affected because of my actions, I had to let bygones be bygones for their sake but it just wasn't that easy.

I kissed her forehead," Shay I promise from this day forward that I will let everything that has happened be a part of the past and I will try my hardest not to look back at it."

She smiled, "Good baby, God will take care of the things that are not in our power to change."

My conscious was killing me because I knew I was bound to break my promise. I couldn't see myself just letting everything Trina had done go. I definitely couldn't let that stunt her cousin pulled rest especially since he wanted to place threats on my head. I wasn't about to let my thoughts take me to a place that I didn't want to be. I just wanted to enjoy my time with Shay; revenge would just have to wait………..

Surprising both of us, my mom poked her head through the door, "I hope I'm not intruding."

Shay smiled," Of course not Ms. King!"

My mom kissed me on the cheek then walked around to the other side of the bed and handed Shay some flowers," I just wanted to stop by to see how you were holding up."

Shay grabbed her hand," Thank you for the flowers. I'm alright, I've seen better days but God has kept me alive."

My mama nodded," Yes honey! Well I just wanted to say hello, I'm going to head on home. Anthony come and walk me to my car baby."

I kissed Shay," I'll be by to see you tomorrow; I'm going to head home too."

Shay smiled," Okay baby, I'll see you later. Thanks again Ms. King!"

My mama hugged Shay," No problem. I hope you feel better."

My mom wrapped her arm around my waist and we made our way down the hallway to the elevators. I pushed the down arrow, the elevator took forever to make its way up to us. An old couple stepped off as we waited to get on, I smiled thinking that could be Shay and I one day. When the elevator got to the floor of the lobby my mother finally broke the silence. I knew something was on her mind because any other time she would have been talking my ear off.

Releasing her arm from my waist," Anthony I want you to come to church with me tomorrow."

I hadn't been to church in I don't know how long. God and I weren't always on the up and up but lately I had been calling on him. My mother always tried to get me to accompany her to church but I always turned down the offer. As a kid she kept me in church but when I got older I started to drift away and started going less and less. I couldn't remember the last time I went to church, it probably had been months if not a year. I thought going would be a good idea, I needed to hear the word, and maybe it would help me clear my head. I didn't have anything against church until it dragged on and on for hours. I couldn't stand being in church from early morning until five and six o'clock.

Shrugging my shoulders," Sure, I'll go with you. I'll pick you up tomorrow morning bright and early!"

She kissed my cheek," Alright son and please don't be late. You know I like to arrive on time."

She not only liked to be on time, she liked to be the first one there and the last one to leave," I'll be early mom I know you like to be the first one there."

Lightly slapping my on my back," That's right!"

I waited until my mother pulled off and I headed for the parking lot. For a second I thought someone had stolen my car but then I remembered I was driving the Cadillac. When I got in the car I checked my missed calls and voicemails. Kyrah had called me and left a message. I knew she was returning my call, I was glad she was being cool about the whole situation. I don't think I could deal with a crazy ass baby mama amongst all the other crazy mutha fucka's that I was dealing with. I knew too many people who had crazy baby mama's, pick the wrong woman to have a baby by and she would make your life a living hell.

I dialed my voicemail to listen to the message," Hey Anthony. Sorry I missed your call I was at work. It's almost seven now but I'm at home. Call me when you get a chance I don't care what time it is when you call I'll be awake."

I looked at the radio it was only seven thirty so I decided to call her back. I dialed her number one digit at a time trying to figure out what I was going to say. Kyrah was a real sweetheart but talking to her made me nervous for some reason. I didn't know what to expect from our conversation even though I wasn't expecting anything.

She quickly picked up the phone," Hey Anthony."

I was thrown off guard by her answering so quickly," Hey Kyrah. I just wanted to know if I could come by tomorrow. I thought maybe I could spend some time with Chris or the three of us could grab a burger or something."

Kyrah answered without any hesitation," I think that is a great idea! I don't have to work so we can do dinner. Are you free around five thirty?"

I smiled," That's cool. Just text me your address and I'll see you and little man tomorrow."

She agreed and we ended the phone call. There was so much that I wanted to ask Kyrah and there was so much that I wanted to know about my son. I didn't want to rush into his life but I also didn't want to waste anymore time not knowing him. The thought of having a son finally had settled in my stomach. I wanted to be the best dad possible. I wanted to do things with Chris that my father never did with me. I wanted to take him to his first basketball game. I wanted to throw him his first pitch and watch him make his first basket. There were so many things a man had to teach his son. There were so many things a man shared with his son. My son was only three but I had big plans for his future. No matter what I did or didn't do in his life I would make sure he stayed out of the streets. I would raise him to respect woman and if it was up to me he would never go through half of the pain or drama I went through. I would teach my son from my mistakes and he would be a better man than me.

I set in the hospital parking lot thinking for about thirty minutes. Most of my thoughts revolved around Chris and how I could make up for lost time with him. I checked the time and it was a few minutes after eight. Instead of going to the studio or getting myself into any more trouble I went straight home. I took the freeway home hoping to avoid traffic and lingering trouble that I might run into by taking the street. I parked the car in the driveway and walked across the grass to pick up the newspaper and proceeded to the mailbox to check the mail. There was a bunch of trash mail and one letter that struck my interest, it didn't have a return address and it wasn't sealed. I read the letter out loud to myself.

Dear Anthony,

I know you killed Quan. I haven't gone to the police but don't think that I won't. I want fifty thousand dollars by next Friday. If I don't get my money you can kiss your son and your bitch good bye. Bring the money to the Marriot Hotel off the freeway in Southfield on telegraph, suite 122. There will be a room key at the front desk for you. Don't try any funny shit because we both know my cousin isn't the friendliest person in the world. Come alone and don't even try to come strapped. When I get my money I'll be out of your life forever. If you think I'm playing, try me mother fucka and I'll make sure you never see the light of day again.

It didn't take a genius to figure out who the letter was from. Trina had me too fucked up if she thought I was about to give her a dime. I would rather rot in jail than give that manipulative bitch her way. I wasn't tripping on her, she could do what she wanted but there wasn't any evidence that could link me to the murder so whatever creative story she came up with wouldn't stick. I went into the house and burned the letter. I didn't bother taking a shower or eating I just went straight into my room and got into bed. It's crazy how life works. I drifted to sleep thinking about Kyrah and our son.

I woke up Sunday morning, showered, put on my suit, grabbed a bowl of cereal and headed to my mother's house. When I pulled up she was sitting on the porch in her Sunday's best. She was one of those women that wore a different outfit every Sunday with one of those ridiculous first lady hats. I swear older women didn't think their outfit for church was official until they put on those big ass hats.

She opened the car door," You're on time!"

Fixing my tie,"I told you I would be."

We drove all the way to the church laughing at one of Ricky Smiley's prank calls C.D. I loved hearing my mother laugh because in turn it made me laugh. She had one of those silly outrageously loud laughs; it was a mixture between a duck and a coyote. In a weird way her laugh eased my worries. We pulled up to the church with a few minutes to spare which was expected, I always joked that we arrived before Jesus. When we stepped into the church it seemed like my mother knew everyone and their grandmother. I was so tired of shaking people's hands and getting kissed on the cheek by old women with hairy upper lips. She introduced me as her baby boy, it was funny since I towered over everyone but I was still my mama's baby. I remembered a lot of people from when I was kid and went to Sunday school but there were also a lot of people that I had seen at the club or on the block. I never understood how people could club all weekend, smoke weed, drink and fuck everything walking but end up at church just to do the same thing the following day. Church and club goers were the biggest contradiction to me but who was I to judge. I was sitting in church contemplating murder.

When my mother was done with her meet and greet we found two seats in the first pew. I sat quietly as my mother turned to the woman next to her and chatted until the pastor took his place. When the pastor started speaking it was as if he was speaking directly to me. I felt lifted by his words, it felt like he was saying everything that I needed to hear. Towards the end of service a woman joined the pastor and asked was there anyone who needed a church home or was there any one that was ready to put their life in God's hands. At first I hesitated but my feet were already in motion when my mind finally caught up. I dropped to my knees and asked the lord to forgive me. I asked him to burn down the bridge I had traveled from and asked him to build another one. The woman rested her hand on my back and prayed. Tears filled my eyes, I felt lifted. The spirit of God had touched my soul. I looked back to see my mother in tears. Her lips mumbled over and over," Thank you God." I closed my eyes and let the woman's voice flow through my body.

She rocked side to side," Lord thank you for bringing this young man to the altar. Thank you for blessing him, continue to walk with him lord. Bless him lord."

The choir began singing as other young men and women gathered around me at the altar. For the first time in a long time I didn't feel alone. Although we all had walked different paths in life we were all up there for the same reason, we wanted and needed forgiveness. The Lord had taken over my body and washed my sins away at that moment I decided everything that had happened no longer mattered. Being in church made me realize and understand how short life is. Forgiveness rest in the hands of the beholder and as long as I was holding onto grudges I wouldn't be able to move forward with my life. I let the words of the prayer move me; I let the rhythm of the songs flow through my body. God was in my presence and he had forgiven me. I had to forgive myself and those who trespassed against me. Church was just the thing I needed in order to think level headed and clear. As the church service came to an end I was flooded with handshakes, kisses, and hugs. I had been welcomed to the church a million times. It felt good to have joined a church and I knew my mother was pleased with me.

I sat next to my mother as I waited for her to finish up a conversation.

She turned to me," I'm so proud of you Anthony."

I embraced my mother," Thank you mama, I couldn't have done it without you."

She smiled," I just brought you here, you did the rest."

Things in church had settled down and the congregation started to flock through the big metal doors that led to the parking lot. I was one of the first people to reach the parking lot. I smiled and waved at everyone on my way to the car. I knew it would at-least be another ten minutes before my mother made her way to the car so I rolled down the windows and let the sounds of Kenny G flow through my speakers. I could feel myself drifting off but as soon as I shut my eyes I heard my mother's voice. She quickly walked to the car trying to avoid anyone else who would trap her into answering a million questions. Church was nice but once service was over I was ready to leave, I didn't need to engage in any extra prayers or conversations. As soon as she got into the car I wasted no time driving off.

Fastening her seatbelt," What are you going to do today?"

I smiled," I'm going to spend some time with Kyrah and Chris."

Her face lit up," I want to meet my grandson!"

I turned onto the lodge," You will mama. I plan on making them both a part of my life."

Rolling the window up," Take care of your son and keep his mother in the picture as well but don't forget that you have a good woman who loves you."

I nodded," I know ma."

Once again my mother had called me out on my shit. I knew it was going to be hard having a son and dealing with his mother along with having a girlfriend but hearing her say it made it so real. Although Shay wasn't the type of woman to get caught up on other females this time it would be different. I wasn't sure about how Kyrah felt about me but I would have to make it clear that our past is history and we wouldn't be tampering with it. I also didn't know how being around Kyrah would make me feel.

Once I dropped my mama off I cruised down Woodward searching for the address Kyrah had given me. I passed several condos before I found her last name on the mailbox. I pulled into the parking lot and shut off the engine. For some reason I was nervous and had to talk myself into walking up the three steps that led to her condo to ring the door bell. My palms were sweating and my finger trembled as I extended my arm to ring the door bell. I could hear movement on the other side of the door, a few seconds later Kyrah stood before me holding Chris in her arms.

She smiled," Sorry about that, I was trying to find his shoes, come on in!"

I laughed," It's cool, I wasn't out there long."

Shutting the door," Make yourself at home, turn on the TV if you want. I'll be right back."

I sat down on the couch and scoped out her place. Pictures of her and Chris were hung along the walls. Everything was neatly arranged and the smell of vanilla filled the air. She had done well for herself, from what I could see the condo looked pretty big and it was well furnished. She had Chris's toys neatly put away in the corner and all his coloring books were neatly stacked on the bookshelf. I was glad that she had made a nice home for herself and Chris without my help; she certainly wasn't like most women looking for a hand out. My eyes wondered to Kyrah as she returned to the living room. She wore black shorts, a wife beater, and some flip flops. I couldn't help but stare at her beauty. I was intrigued by her rich brown complexion and her thick thighs. When we kicked it back in the day she was bony and had no extravagant features. As I looked upon her luscious curves I noticed a lot had changed since then, Kyrah had grown into a beautiful woman. When she smiled small dimples appeared that added a sense of innocents to her beauty.

Her gentle voice broke me from my thoughts," I'm so glad that you decided to come over!"

Smiling," I am too! I was thinking we could go to Fuddruckers and then maybe to the park or something."

She nodded," That sounds like a plan to me. I just need to find his other shoe then we can go. Do you mind putting that stuff next to you in his backpack?"

"No problem." I began placing the items from the couch into the small Ninja Turtle backpack.

When Kyrah finally found Chris's shoe we headed for the front door. Kyrah took a double take to make sure we had everything then turned on the alarm as we rushed out the door. I hooked Chris's car seat into the back of the car and buckled him in securely. Kyrah smiled as I managed to do everything without her assistance. It wasn't my first time being around a child, so I wasn't completely clueless about how to handle a car seat. Kyrah and I talked the whole time to the restaurant but Chris had passed out as soon as we pulled off.

Placing the car in park," He must be tired."

Removing her seatbelt," He falls asleep whenever he is in a moving car. Up until he was a year old I would have to take him for a ride inorder for him to fall asleep."

I smiled," I'll carry him in; I know kids are cranky when they first wake up."

She giggled," Tell me about it!"

When Kyrah talked about Chris she did it with such excitement and she kept a huge smile on her face. He was definitely her world and I admired that. I unbuckled Chris and placed him on my shoulder. His little body was so warm. As soon as I had him wrapped in my arms he woke up and ran his face across my shoulder then wrapped his arms around my neck. I whispered for him to go back to sleep. He stared at me for a few seconds then plopped his head back down. Kyrah trailed next to me digging through her purse, I chuckled to myself as she dug with intensity. The restaurant was so hectic it wasn't really the surrounding I was expecting but I guess no restaurant would be quaint and quiet. I held Chris in my arms until the noise woke him up completely. His eyes lit up when he saw all the race car games and other kids. I could feel his small body wiggling to get free. I bent down and waited for his feet to touch the ground before I loosened my grip.

He tugged on Kyrah's leg and pointed," Can I play mommy."

She nodded," Yes."

Chris wasn't the average three year old, he was smart and very independent for his age. I could tell Kyrah was raising him with a stern but gentle hand. He wasn't one of those three year olds that still wore pampers or that needed you to hold his hand every second of the day. It surprised me how well he could speak and how smart he was. When I was three I just wanted to watch TV all day and eat cereal.

Kyrah and I found a table and ordered our food. We both kept Chris in our eye sight as we settle down to eat. Kyrah was so easy to talk to, I loved that in a woman. We talked about all that had been going on and she even asked me about Shay and my family. I guess I was expecting her to have pent up anger against me but it was the complete opposite. She was truly a sweetheart. Part of me wanted to kiss her but the other part of me blocked out my feelings because I was in a relationship with Shay. Everything felt so right and I felt open to her. Thankfully Chris ran up to the table looking for food which drenched whatever flames were lit between us. I let out a sigh of relief because honestly I don't know how much longer I could fight my feelings. Kyrah settled Chris into the chair next to her and fixed his plate. For him to be so small he had a big appetite. I watched as Kyrah took such care and interest in him. My heart was opening up to both of them. It was hard for me not to love them both. Her laugh and gentle touch alone made my heart beat fast. I wasn't sure what was going on with me but I liked the feeling. After we finished our food I paid the check and we headed up the street to the park. Chris darted to the playground as Kyrah and I settled on a park bench and watched all the kids play.

I laughed," Isn't it crazy how kids can just play with other kids they don't even know and not think twice about it."

She smiled," At their age everything is simple. It doesn't matter what you look like or what you have. Nothing matters but having fun."

I knew what we were talking about but I felt guilty. I felt like she was referring to me when we were younger. I sat there silently trying to drown out my own thoughts.

Resting her head on my shoulder," Anthony today has been really nice."

I wrapped my arm around her," Yeah it has been."

For that moment I forgot about everything that had been going on, I forgot about Shay and Trina. I forgot about Mike and I even forgot about how I had killed Quan. I was lost in the moment, I was actually happy. I lifted her face up with my finger and kissed her. I knew the park was full of people but when our lips met it was like we were the only two people on the planet. Her lips were so soft and warm, I felt a strong connection between us.

Pulling back," What about your girlfriend?"

Placing my finger over her lip," I'll worry about her."

I knew who I wanted to be with. I felt guilty because I had put Shay through so much but I couldn't hide my feelings. A blind man could see that I wanted to be with Kyrah and my son. My mother's warning didn't stick. Shay had helped me be a better man but I couldn't help but think that Kyrah could help me be a great man, the man I needed to be in order to raise my son.

Wrapping her fingers through mine," I don't want you making hasty decisions. I know you love Shay and I don't want to break up your happy home. I also don't want to complicate your life anymore than it already is."

Kissing her forehead," I'm not making any hasty decisions. I just want to be with my son. I know I have a girlfriend but today has been special with no effort and that tells me there is something between us. I know I did you wrong in the past but I would never do it again. I've changed and I know I put you through hell but just give me one more chance."

She stared into my eyes," If this is really what you want, okay. All of our days won't be like this. Raising a child isn't always a walk in the park. If you're going to be a part of our lives, then you're in it for the long run. You walked out on me once but I won't have that again. If your with me your with me and no one else. We have a son together but that doesn't mean we have to be together. I would love to be with you but not if you only want to be together because of Chris."

I pulled her closer to my chest," Today has showed me what I've been missing out on. I want to be in our son's life but I also want to be in yours."

She smiled," I think we both would like that."

I had made my decision now I had to figure out how I was going to tell Shay. She was the main one getting hurt in the whole process. I didn't want to hurt her but I had to go with my heart and my heart beat to Kyrah's drum. There is nothing worse than being with someone and thinking about someone else. I decided that I would go to the hospital in the morning and lay all my cards out on the table. She probably would hate me when it was all said and done but at least she would know the truth. I never would intentionally hurt Shay and eventually she would understand that.

It was starting to get dark so we headed back to Kyrah's. Chris was worn out; all his energy was gone. I carried him to his room and placed him in the bed. I sat on the side of his bed and watched as he slept. I kissed his small hand and closed the door behind me. Kyrah was leaning up against the wall in the hallway waiting for me.

Hugging me," Thank you for today!"

Embracing her warmth," Anytime sweetheart. When can we do this again?"

She smiled," Anytime, hopefully this will become a regular thing for the three of us!"

Placing a small kiss on her neck," Me too!"

She began to kiss and suck on my neck as my hands explored her body. Before I knew it, I could feel her erect nipples pointing through her shirt. My dick was throbbing as it pressed against my pants. She nibbled on my ear which drove me crazy. We backed up and fell onto the couch and her body landed on top of mine. I knew she wanted me as bad as I wanted her. She began to unbutton my shirt as I slipped my hand into her panties to feel her wetness oozing from between her juicy thighs. We both knew what we were about to do was wrong because I still had a girlfriend and I didn't want either of us to rush into anything. She didn't mention having a boyfriend but either way I just didn't want to intrude into her life with sex.

I removed my hand from her panties," I have to go."

She lifted herself up," Why?"

Buttoning my shirt," I don't want to rush this. I really want us to work and this isn't the right way to start off."

She nodded," I understand."

We moved to separate ends of the couch staring at each other with desire. I had to think about something that turned me off because otherwise I would have had her screaming my name in thirty different languages. The way she bit her bottom lip teased my erect dick even more. I wanted to make love to her more than anything but I couldn't betray Shay any further than I had already done.

I fidgeted for a second," Okay let me head home I need to hit the studio for a while."

She stood up," Okay, call me later if you feel like talking."

Looking around making sure I had all my belongings," Okay baby girl I had a good time today!"

Wrapping her arms around my neck," I did too!"

We stood in a long embrace; I kissed her cheek and headed for the door. I didn't expect for us to get close so soon but with the way my life had been going, I wasn't surprised.

Chapter Ten

The next few days seemed to have flown by. Shay was out of the hospital and I still hadn't mentioned my lack of faith in our relationship. My main focus was getting her well and helping her regain her strength. I hadn't told anyone what had almost happened between Kyrah and I. The things that happened between me and Kyrah would have to remain low key until we both came to a conclusion about exactly what we wanted. I continued to visit Chris but any sexual tension between me and Kyrah was suppressed for the moment. For the last few days Trina had been leaving me threatening messages but I didn't pay them any attention. She was stupid and wasn't worth worrying about. Clearly if she tried anything slick I had all the messages to prove that she was out to get me. Even though she had Quan's murder dangling over my head she lacked solid evidence and I had the upper hand because she portrayed herself as a stalker and crazy ex lover. For the moment my life was partially normal, nobody had been trying to kill me and it appeared that things between Mike and I were squashed. Mike and I both had come to terms that we were going to be in each other's lives whether we liked it or not. Out of respect for Kyrah we came to a mutual understanding, we would tolerate each other even if we didn't like one another. I had even gotten Shawn to lay low. Life was good but good things don't last forever.

Friday seemed to come rather quickly, I wasn't sure of what the outcome would be after meeting with Trina. I prepared myself for the worst case scenario because I wasn't sure what Trina was capable of. Although I wasn't worried about her crazy ass, I was worried about my families' safety. I gave Kyrah some money to get away for the weekend, so she took Chris and drove out to her cousins' house in Chicago. In case the law got involved I had Jim's number on speed dial and I filled Tone in on everything in case shit turned deadly on my behalf. Whatever Trina had up her sleeve I would be semi prepared for it. It was a little past noon as I headed to the hotel. I would roll over in my grave twice before I gave Trina anymore of my money so I didn't bother going to the bank to withdraw her request for cash. When I got to the hotel I took everything out my pockets except for my keys and cell phone. I wasn't about to be caught carrying a weapon or any other shit that could get my ass locked up. I strolled into the hotel lobby trying to go unnoticed. I learned as a child to blend in, it makes it harder for someone to point you out if the shit hit the fan.

I arrived at the front desk," Excuse me someone left a room key for me and I'm here to pick it up."

The gentleman smiled," No problem! I just need the name on the room's account and your last name."

Clearing my throat," I believe it's under a Ms. Trina Whitfield and my name is King."

Typing in the name on his computer," Yes, room 122 it is on the third floor the sixth room to your left. Ms. Whitfield has already checked in. Here is your key, enjoy your stay!"

Placing the key in my pocket," Thank you."

I avoided the commotion of the elevator and took the stairs. I got to the third floor and my heart began to pound a million miles per second. With one foot in front of the other I got closer and closer to the room. I pulled the key out my pocket and placed it in the door. Trina was sitting on the bed watching Jerry Springer when I walked in. I looked around the room before I shut the door, nothing seemed suspicious or out of order.

She laughed," Nigga nobody is here but you and me."

I shook my head," Well I don't know what I'm walking into all that shit you were talking in that letter and those messages."

Turning off the TV," Ant, I don't want your money or need it. I had to threaten you to see you because I knew if I would have asked you to come here you wouldn't have."

I leaned against the wall," You're damn right, so what is it that you want?"

She walked towards me," I want you. I want you to leave that prissy bitch and I want us to be together. She isn't as perfect as you think she is, ask your brother."

I walked around her," Stop playing games. I'm tired of this back and forth shit. You sent your cousin and his yes man after me and think we can still be together? I don't ever want to be in the same room as you again."

Throwing her hands up," I admit sticking my cousin on you was ridiculous and I've apologized for all the drama. I've had a lot of time to think and you're a good man. I just want to be with you. I'll even quit working at the club; it will just be you and me!"

I laughed," Trina you just don't get it. It will never be just you and me because your full of secrets and you don't know what you want. I'm trying to do right by my family but it seems like with you around that isn't possible. I'm sorry, you and me will never exist. Even when it was supposed to be you and me, it wasn't. Old flames die hard. "

She plopped down on the bed," Please leave."

I respected her wishes and headed for the door.

As I was closing the door she shouted," Fuck you, you're going to regret this nigga, believe that."

I laughed," That is exactly the shit I'm talking about."

I slammed the door and took the stairs to the lobby. I gave the room key back to the man at the front desk and headed to my car. The words Trina spoke circled through my head," Ask your brother." I couldn't help but wonder exactly what she meant by that. I couldn't sweat the situation because after all the shit I had put Shay through I couldn't question her about something that did or didn't happen between her and my brother. Either way it hadn't happened in the last few weeks while we were together so it wasn't any of my business, even though I didn't like the idea of the two of them sleeping together. Shay was a good woman but Trina was right I did have her ass on a pedestal like she could do no wrong. As I pulled out of the hotel parking lot into the busy traffic I drowned my thoughts with the sound of passing cars.

A few weeks had passed and I finally worked up the courage to talk to Shay. I walked up the front steps to her house and I could feel my heart rate speeding up. I wanted to go back to the way things were with her but the truth was things between her and I would never be the same. I had to face the music, the relationship we had wasn't as perfect as either of us thought. The last thing I wanted to do was hurt her but I had to tell her all the things I was holding back. Swallowing my fear I rung the doorbell and waited for her to open the door.

Unlocking the screen door," Hey."

Looking at my feet," Hey Shay."

She tugged at my shirt," What's the matter?'

I sat in one of the lawn chairs that were pushed up against the house," We need to talk."

Her facial expression showed signs of confusion," About what Ant?"

I patted my lap for her to sit down," I need to tell you something and I don't want you getting upset."

She nodded.

Taking in a breath of air," Shay you know I love you but right now I'm a little confused. I've been spending a lot of time with Kyrah and I'm starting to catch feelings for her. I love being around her and my son, it feels so right. I don't want either of you getting hurt so I think we need to take a break."

Folding her arms," I can understand you wanting to be with your son and trying to work things out with his mother so I won't stand in the way. I saw this coming so I can't even be upset. I have something I need to tell you as well."

My eyebrow rose in suspicion," What about?"

Tears streamed from her eyes," This happened a long time ago. Tone and I slept together once. I was going to your mom's house to drop your stuff off and you weren't there but he was. We went to the basement and one thing led to another, we ended up having sex. We both knew it was a mistake so we decided not to tell you. Trina has been calling my phone threatening that she was going to tell you and I would rather have it come from my mouth opposed to hers."

I shrugged it off," Is that all?"

Shaking her head," Yes, that's all."

Rubbing my hand across her thigh," I'm not tripping off the two of you sleeping together. I appreciate you telling me. It happened a minute ago and after all the shit I've put you through I would be a straight asshole to nut up on you about that."

She smiled," I'm glad you understand. I know it hurts you to know that I was with your brother but it wasn't intentionally and it didn't mean anything."

Looking at my watch," I understand. Let's put all that behind us. I hate to leave in a rush but I have to take Kyrah to work."

Shay's face dropped," Oh.......Alright."

Removing herself from my lap," Bye."

Before I could say bye she walked in the house and shut the door. I knew she was pissed because I was leaving her to go to Kyrah. Shay said she understood but I knew that her feelings were still hurt. I left the situation alone because we both needed time to cool off. I played it off like I didn't care that she had been with Tone but deep down inside it really hurt me. I could deal with the fact that it happened but she never would have told me if it wasn't for Trina threatening her. I always tried to keep an honest relationship with her but her keeping that secret made me think about what else she could be hiding. It wasn't in my character to force shit from a person so my mind would just be full of curiosity, I guess everyone has untellable secrets. I let the bullshit fly away in the wind and I proceeded to Kyrah's house.

When I pulled up Kyrah was standing on the porch. Before I could even put the car in park she was standing at the door waiting for me to hit the unlock button. She looked so good in her little work uniform with her hair pulled to the back in a neat ponytail.

I smiled," Damn is there something exciting at work waiting for you."

She laughed," Hell yeah it's pay day!"

Laughing," Oh, well shit let me hurry up and get you there!"

Giggling," Shut up big head. I just want to be on time. Since my sister has been borrowing my car I've been late all week."

Pushing in a CD," You need to get your shit back from her ass."

Digging through her purse," Yea, I know but she is trying to find a new place so I'm trying to be patient with her."

Being in Kyrah's presence made my minor attitude and headache from Shay disappear. She was so funny; she kept me laughing the entire ride to her job. Unlike Shay, Kyrah didn't take everything so serious; she took things as they came and didn't worry about the little things. The more we laughed and talked the more I knew I wanted to be with her.

Stopping at a red light," Kyrah I want us to be together. I want us to raise our child together. I want to wake up next to you every day. I want us to be a family."

She smiled," I thought Shay was the person you were supposed to spend the rest of your life with? I thought she was supposed to have your kids? Ya'll play the bestfriend game but I see the way you look at each other."

Directing my attention to the road," That's what I thought until I got a chance to spend time with you and our son. I talked to Shay earlier and told her we needed to take a break. No doubt I love Shay, I will always love her but we are better as friends. Shay will always be near and dear to my heart but I see things in you that I don't see in her. I want to see our son grow up and I want to be by your side while I do that. I want him to have a dad; I want to be the dad that mine never was. I want to be your man and not just your baby daddy. One day in the near future I want to put a ring on your finger and spend the rest of my days with you and only you."

Watching cars pass," Anthony, that all sounds like a beautiful plan but like I said I don't want Chris to be the reason your with me. I also know you love Shay and I know it will be hard for the both of you to just walk away from each other and I'm not going to play the break up to make up game with you."

I laughed," The break up to make up game, huh? Shay and I have been in and out of a relationship and we have also been friends since we were kids but our history together will not interfere with the future I'm trying to build with you. I won't lie, I love Shay and I always will but the love I have for you has become stronger. I know where you're coming from but Chris isn't the only reason I want to be with you."

Kyrah looked at me," I know you both have been on a love roller coaster since you were kids. I doubt it is completely over between the two of you but it is what it is. Since Chris isn't the only reason you want to be with me, why do you want to be with me?"

I sighed," Your smart, intelligent, beautiful, caring, you turn my bad moods into good ones without effort. I love your laugh and your gentle touch. You're independent and a hard working woman. I enjoy every second I spend with you and you're the mother of my first born."

Placing her hand on my cheek," Anthony I want to make a life with you but I need to know that you won't just walk out on Chris and me to be with Shay or any other woman. I need to know that it's just us. Take a few days and if building a future with me is still what you want then we will move forward from there but if it isn't than just be a father to Chris."

I agreed.

Kyrah was an understanding woman but she was also demanding. I did need some time to think and I had to assure the both of us that I was over Shay. Shay had been the only woman I had really cared about so it made it hard to just walk away from her but I needed to focus on Chris and trying to build a life with him and Kyrah was a part of that life. I would always love Shay but Kyrah and I had more to build on but on the other hand Shay and I had already been through so much. I felt like I owed both of them something.

She pointed," You can let me out here."

Placing the car in park," Have a good day!"

She smiled and gave me a kiss," Thank you! Are you going to pick me up?"

Nodding," What time do you get off?"

Playing with her phone," I work overnight today, so my shift ends at 10 A.M. tomorrow."

Adjusting my hat," Yea, I'll be here."

We embraced in a long hug than she strolled into the nursing home entrance. As I pulled off I missed her already. Kyrah had always been a sweetheart I was just too stupid back in the day to realize it. I headed straight to the studio to meet up with Mack and Trigger. I knew my music had been slacking so I needed to meet up with them and start getting myself and my music back on track. We cracked jokes with each other then got straight to business.

Mack always said," There is nothing funny about losing money, money talks and if you're broke nobody is listening."

I hit the booth hard making up for all the days that I had neglected my music. When we finally left the studio it was two in the morning. Trigger and I had worked on a song together and I finished recording a song that I had started a few months ago. I felt good about the progress we had made.

Chapter Eleven

The next few weeks went by smoothly, Shay and I had decided that we would just remain friends because things were too complicated to try and work on a relationship. We talked as if nothing had ever happened we were back to being best-friends. We would always be each other's first loves but our love story was over. It was time for us both to move on and build lives with other people. Kyrah and I had been taking baby steps towards a relationship and I was happier than ever. We spent almost every night together, I felt like I had the world in my palms. I thought my momma was going to be upset that Shay and I broke up but she was happy that Kyrah and I were trying to work things out. She didn't like the idea of Kyrah being my baby momma and Shay being my girlfriend, she said I had too much going on. Tone tried to bring up the situation between him and Shay but I told him to let it ride, he would always be my brother nothing or anybody would ever change that. Going to the studio had become a part of my everyday routine again so my money was flowing in consistently. It's funny how one minute things can go so well then everything just falls apart.

For the last two days someone had been calling my phone and hanging up. I disregarded it until Kyrah noticed that there was always a red car parked in the complex where she lived, that she had never seen before but whenever she turned on the porch lights they would pull off. In the beginning I figured it was just some kids fooling around but it was happening to frequently. I didn't know anyone with a red car so I didn't stress the situation but it was odd that both things were happening at the same time. Kyrah became so frantic that she and Chris began staying at my house until we could figure out what was going on. I enjoyed them being around every day, it felt like we were really a family. My house was always so quiet unless I was down in the studio or a game was on but with them around it was filled with laughter and love.

One night we were all having dinner and someone knocked on the door. When I went to the door no one was there and I didn't see any cars.

Kyrah asked," Who was at the door babe?"

I shrugged," I don't know. Nobody was out there."

Kyrah twisted her face," I really think we need to get away for a while. Too many suspicious things have been happening lately."

I sat down and continued eating," I'm not going to run. If someone wants me or you they will just follow us."

After I said that I wish I hadn't.

She slammed her glass on the table," Well I won't wait around for someone to harm me or my son."

I dropped my fork in my plate," I wouldn't just sit around and let something happen to you or our son."

She shook her head," Well it doesn't seem that way besides you aren't Super Man you can't save everybody."

I looked at Chris then back to her," Kyrah I promise that I will protect you and our son. Super Man ain't got shit on me."

She smiled," I know!"

Her frantic mind frame was starting to make me paranoid. I made sure my gun was loaded and tucked away at all times. I made sure all the doors were double locked and the alarm was on when we were sleep or gone. I couldn't remember the last time I had even used my alarm system. There was only so much I could do to ensure our safety anything else was left in the hands of fate.

Tone agreed to stay with Kyrah and Chris while I went to see Shawn. I hadn't been in contact with him much every since Kyrah and I had been playing house. When I got to his house it felt like old times. We smoked a few blunts, ate, and played Madden. It was nice to get away for a while and just be a guy instead of a daddy and a boyfriend even though I loved being both. Shawn understood that times were changing. We were both walking in two different paths of life. His business was in the streets still and mine was with my music and family. No doubt we would always be boys but our life styles were too different, they would eventually clash. I mentioned what had been going on with the strange phone calls and cars, he told me to watch my back. I didn't take that lightly. I wasn't sure if he had heard something or he was just looking out for me but either way I was on guard. When weird shit is going on and you don't know who is behind it you tend to not trust anybody. Shawn was my boy and I trusted him but I still was on guard around him. I always kept in the back of my mind that it's only a matter of time before friends turn into enemies.

Placing the controller down," Ok nigga I'm about to raise up."

Shawn released smoke from his lips," Fa sho. Keep your head up bro."

Nodding," You do the same."

As I pulled out of Shawn's driveway my phone rang. It was another one of the hang up calls I had been receiving. This cat and mouse game was starting to get real annoying. I proceeded to a stop light on the corner of my street when my phone rang again. I didn't bother looking at it. When I pulled into the driveway Chris was playing in the yard with Tone and Kyrah was reading a magazine on the porch.

Chris dropped his toys," Daddy!"

I picked him up," Hey little man! Are you having fun with your uncle Tone?"

Hugging my neck tightly," Yes!"

I smiled," Good!"

Tone gathered the toys from the grass," Wad up bro?"

Putting Chris down," Nothing same old bullshit."

He laughed," I feel you. Things were pretty quite around here today."

Letting out a sigh of relief," Good looking bro."

He nodded," You know I got you."

Chris and Tone continued to play while Kyrah and I went into the house for a little quickie. As soon as we went into my bedroom I heard gunshots. I grabbed my gun and told her to stay in the house. When I went outside a red car swerved off. I looked around and didn't see anything when I looked a little further I saw Tone on the ground. My heart thumped loudly as I got closer to my brother. Blood was coloring the side walk red at a rapid rate. From the looks of it Tone had jumped in front of Chris to save him from the bullets. Tears rushed from my eyes as I gripped his hand.

He gasped for his last breathe," It was that cop."

A few minutes later his body lay limp on the ground, I knew he was dead. My hands trembled as I closed his eyelids. Chris was screaming and crying. Kyrah came running out the house with 911 on the phone. I lost my mind for a second and starting punching the concrete, my knuckles began to bleed but I didn't care. I could feel them starting to burn but I just kept swinging.

Kyrah wrapped her arms around me as tears filled her eyes," Baby stop."

I looked down at Tone's lifeless body and tears flowed heavily down my face, my brother was gone. When the police arrived they flooded us with questions. In my mind every police officer was dirty just like the mutha fucka who shot my brother. I sat on the porch silent as Kyrah stood strong for me and answered their questions. My mind raced as I thought about how I would tell my mother that her son had just been murdered. It was my mother's worst fear that another one of her children would be killed; no parent should have to bury their child. I sat on the porch until the morgue arrived. They put a sheet over him and rolled him into a body bag. I watched as they placed him in the back of the black van and drove away.

One of the officers patted me on my shoulder," Sir I'm sorry about your brother here are his belongings. You should really have one of the medics look at your hands."

Ignoring his suggestion, I opened the bag and went through the things. There was a picture of Tone and me from when we were kids, a picture of our sisters and momma, some money, his watch, cell phone, and a gold chain that our grandmother had given him before she died. I tucked the bag into my pocket and pulled out my phone. I called Shawn and told him what happened, he was on his way before I even finished the story. When he pulled up I asked him to stay with Kyrah and Chris so I could go see my momma.

He agreed," Give momma King my love."

I nodded.

I drove below the speed limit trying to delay the trip but no matter how slow I drove I got to my mother's house quicker than usual. I pulled into the driveway and shut the engine off. I wiped my face and tried to maintain my composure. I knocked on the door softly. When my mother opened the door she immediately knew something was wrong. I looked at her once and tears streamed down my face.

She grabbed my hands," What is the matter baby, what happened to your knuckles?"

I dropped to my knees," He's dead momma. He's dead."

She looked confused," Who baby? Who is dead?"

Trying to fight back my tears," Tone."

She let out a loud scream," No, not my Tone, not my baby."

I stood up and wrapped her in my arms. We both stood on the front porch crying trying to console each other. This was the second time I would have to bury one of my brothers. I wasn't really close to my oldest brother who had been killed a few years back but Tone was my right hand man, he was my bestfriend. Knowing that he was dead made me feel like a piece of me went with him. Once we pulled ourselves together she wanted to know what happened. I didn't know anymore than she did and that made it hurt even more.

I cleared my throat," He was outside in the front yard with Chris playing while Kyrah and I were in the house. I heard gunshots and rushed outside. He was on the ground and blood was everywhere. Before he died he took his last breathe and told me it was that cop that had arrested me on those bogus charges. He died saving my son's life."

I could tell she was trying to stomach the information," The same cop that is Trina's cousin?"

I nodded," Yes. Don't worry mama I'm going to handle it."

She looked up at me," Anthony, no you won't. I won't lose two sons in one day. You just worry about taking care of Kyrah and Chris. Let God work this one out."

I shook my head," No mama, I have to handle this for Tone, that should have been me."

Slamming her hand on the table," Dammit, boy let it rest. You can't just go around killing folks thinking that will make your problems go away. Your brother is dead and killing someone else isn't going to bring him back. When will you realize that shooting people doesn't solve anything, it only makes matters worse. I wanted better for you boys."

I reached into my pocket and gave her the bag of Tone's belongings," I thought you might like to have this."

Tears filled her eyes as she searched through the bag and looked at its contents. She pulled my grandmothers necklace from the bag and placed it around my neck," I think your brother would have liked for you to have this."

I smiled," Momma pray for us."

She grabbed my chin," I always do. Tone is in God's hands so I know he is alright and we will be alright too."

My mother and I sat in silence as she rested her head on my shoulder. We had cried all the tears we could cry in a day. Our hearts had been ripped from our chest. I struggled with the idea of never seeing Tone again as she struggled with the idea of her second oldest son being gone. We made a few phone calls to family members and the house slowly started to fill. My sisters took the news pretty hard but they managed to hold their composure. Tone's girlfriend showed up and she was devastated. Although my brother lived for the streets he had a lot of people who loved him. He had numerous friends and family members that mourned his death. My mother called one of her friends to spend the night with her. I appreciated the fact that so many people loved and respected my brother and the man that he was. When the house was cleared I decided to head home, I knew Chris and Kyrah were probably pretty shook up.

My mother hugged me for what seemed like forever," Anthony please don't do anything stupid. Be careful and try to get some sleep. I love you!"

Fighting tears," I won't mama and I don't think sleep is in the forecast. I love you too and I will see you in the morning."

I hugged her friend," Take care of my mama."

She smiled," I will Anthony; everything is going to be alright."

I walked to my car and broke down in tears again. All day everyone was telling me that everything was going to be okay but my brother was dead, how in the fuck was everything going to be okay? I thought about that cop and I thought about Trina. My heart was in shambles. I should have been the one in the morgue; I should have been the one protecting my son. Tone was always the one trying to protect me; he was the one always looking out for me but who was looking out for him? Most people didn't know what it was like to have a big brother like him. As kids if I ever got into trouble with my mama he would always bring me an ice cream and tell me to stop crying. Since our dad wasn't around and my other brother was always in and out of prison he was the man of the house. Everyone was telling me that it was going to be ok but Tone was more than a brother he was the closest thing I had to a dad. I hadn't just lost a brother, I lost a piece of myself.

When I pulled up to my house Kyrah rushed to the car," I was so worried about you."

I embraced her," I'm okay."

Shawn came outside holding Chris's hand," Do you want me to stay over?"

Kyrah smiled," Could you?"

Scratching his head," Of course."

I picked Chris up," Thank you man."

Shawn looked me in the eyes," You know you're my brother and so was Tone. Whatever you need I'm here no questions asked."

We all walked into the house and tried to settle down for the night. Although the house was quiet nobody was getting much sleep. Chris laid inbetween Kyrah and me tossing and turning, Kyrah and I lay staring into each other's eyes. She tried to get me to talk about how I felt, I didn't feel like talking but I certainly didn't feel like talking about my feelings. My feelings were numb, I felt dead and empty inside. She wasn't very close to Tone but I knew she was hurting because I was hurting. It's crazy how loving a person can make you feel everything that they feel. I wanted so badly to just get dressed, load my gun, and go kill Trina and her cousin but my mother was right killing people wasn't going to solve anything. I had killed Quan and that certainly didn't solve anything. The whole situation had gotten out of hand. I was confused and didn't know what to do. I had no evidence to take to the police and the only witness was dead. I was stuck and I had run out of things to do.

Chapter Twelve

The next morning wasn't any better. My head felt like it weighed fifty pounds and my stomach was in knots. Chris was so scared that he wanted Kyrah or me by his side at all times. Kyrah was still standing strong for me and made sure Chris was taken care of so I could have sometime to myself. Shawn had been holding down the household answering the door and taking messages if anyone called. I didn't feel like eating and I wasn't in the mood for company. I locked myself in the studio and did what I knew how to do best. It took me seven hours to write and record the perfect song. I wrote the song in remembrance of Tone. It was about being brothers and our journey through life. As the song flowed through my ears tears dripped from my eyes. I poured everything I had into the song, every dose of sadness and anger. It was almost eight minutes long, a summary of my twenty two years being Tones little brother.

I had cried so much that my eyes burned. When Kyrah knocked on the door I wiped my face and headed up the steps. I opened the door, I knew she could tell that I had been crying but she didn't say anything she just wiped my eyes and wrapped her arms around my neck. I felt so warm with her body pressed against mine that for a minute I believed everything was going to be okay but when she released me from her embrace I snapped back into reality.

Trying to lighten the mood," So we are all starving and you need to eat so what do you say we go get some food and maybe we can go catch a movie or something. We all need to have some fun and we all need some fresh air."

Forcing a smile," That sounds good. Let me just call my mom first."

Kyrah took Chris by the hand and walked outside to sit on the porch, Shawn followed behind them. I picked up the phone and dialed my mother's number. Her voice sent comfort through my body. She sounded as if she was holding up okay but she was worried about me. I assured her that I was alright. We discussed a few details about the funeral arrangements and the arrangements for our out of state family members. I was shocked when she told me that my father had called, pigs would fly if he actually showed his face at the funeral. When we ended the phone call I could feel myself falling apart again but instead I chose to shake it off and join my family outside. Nothing seemed to be the same, the world seemed colder and the sun didn't seem as bright. Even though Kyrah and Shawn tried their best to keep my attention away from the death of Tone it didn't work. We ended up eating at Starters which was where Tone and I had shared many drinks and laughs. After dinner we drove through Belle Isle. As I pushed Chris on the swing, I remembered the days when Tone and I would ride our bikes through the park and spend hour's playing basketball or trying to talk to all the older women in the park. The city was just full of his memories. As the night came to an end I found myself questioning my life. I could only question why God took my brother away instead of me when I was the reason behind all the madness. I felt like I didn't deserve to live.

The day of the funeral arrived quicker than I expected. I tried to prepare myself but nothing could prepare me for saying goodbye to my brother. I hated funerals because they were the final straw, they were the last good-bye. I struggled to get out of bed and get myself together. I gazed in the mirror and my eyes were red and puffy. I needed a haircut, I just wasn't myself. As I turned on the shower and let the warm water run down my body I decided that I would really have to change my life. If I couldn't change for myself I had to do it for the people around me. I finished my shower and shaved in-order to look semi decent. Kyrah rushed back and forth trying to get herself ready as well as Chris. When we were all finally dressed we headed to my mother's house where the limo would pick us up and take us to the church. When we pulled up to the church there were masses of people, I never expected so many people to come and show their respects. I knew my brother was loved but damn it looked like a celebrity funeral. I was grateful that so many people loved my brother and my family to pay us their respects and say their final good-byes. My mother stayed strong until she walked up to the casket. In a matter of seconds she went from being calm to crying out," God why my son?" She reached into the casket and kissed Tone on his cheek. I wrapped her in my arms and we walked slowly back to the pew where we were sitting. One by one people walked up to Tones casket and said their final words. The pastor gave his sermon which brought the whole church to tears. I found the strength to speak to my brother one last time.

The pastor gave his last words," I believe Anthony has something to say about his brother Antonio then the choir will lead us out in song. "

I walked up to the stand," I want to thank each and everyone of you from the bottom of my heart for being here today. I'm sure my brother is smiling right now knowing that he had so many people that loved him. I still can't believe he is gone. I remember as kids we drove our mother crazy, we were always up to something. He protected me and made sure I stayed out of trouble. My brother is and always will be my bestfriend. He lives on in each and every one of us. I love him with all my heart. I'm grateful that he had so many people who loved him, thank you all for being here in these hard times. I will never forget all the times Tone and I shared and I will never forget how much he loved me."

The pianist began to play will you remember me as the choir began to sing. The congregation was full of teary eyes. Everyone gathered outside as we let at least a couple hundred blue and white balloons go into the air, those were his favorite colors. I knew Tone was in a better place but my heart was broken.

After the service everyone joined together at my mother's house, we ate and told stories about Tone. For the first time since Tone died I found a reason to smile and a reason to laugh again. It was easy to smile and laugh surrounded by a group of people who genuinely loved Tone, me, and my family. I knew it would take time but we were all going to be alright. My mother was smiling, so that made me smile. Shay showed up and there was no tension in the air between us or her and Kyrah, they actually sat down and talked to one another for a while. Before Shay left she and I had a chance to talk, like always she was there for me when I needed her most.

Kyrah had been there for me as well but Shay understood how close Tone and I were, she knew my past so it made it easier for me to talk to her about what was going on in my head. Our friendship was defiantly still strong.

Wrapping her arms around me," Call me if you need anything, everything is going to be alright. You know Tone loved you, your mom, and your sisters very much!"

Smiling," Thank you Shay!"

She gently placed her hand on Kyrah's back," Nice talking to you sweetie!"

Kyrah smiled," Nice talking to you too!"

I was happy that we could all be in the same room and act civilized. I expected them to despise one another but I knew they were both better than that and they both had more class to stir up some bullshit on the day of my brothers funeral. No matter what they both would always be two of the most important women in my life. As the group of people started to get smaller and smaller Shawn helped me clean up the mess and put away the food. We put my mother's house back in order and thanked the remaining guest for coming as they began to leave. After everyone left I looked around at all the pictures of Tone. I walked passed each one remembering the days that they were taken. Kyrah came up behind me and placed her arms around my waist. We didn't speak we just looked at the pictures.

My mother cleared her throat," Well kids I think everything turned out alright."

I nodded," Yea me too mama."

We all shared a few more words before we went our separate ways. My mother was holding herself together pretty well and my sisters seemed to be handling the situation pretty well also. It was sad but I think we all expected Tone to get killed sooner or later. Even when you expect something to happen, when it actually happens, it's hard to believe.

Chapter Thirteen

The next few weeks seemed to fly pass, before I knew it a month had passed since the funeral. Things were starting to go back to normal. I was back in the studio on a regular basis getting my album together and focused on my family. I vowed to myself to put my family and friends first from now on. I had been keeping close contact with my sisters and keeping up with what they were doing, my father and I sat down and put the past aside. I forgave him for my own sake, I couldn't hold onto hate forever. I was ready to build a relationship with him, so we could get to know each other. Kyrah and I were becoming extremely close; I was falling in love with her. I tried to maintain contact with Shawn but keep my distance from him at the same time because the streets were still his main focus. Every night I found myself praying, asking God for forgiveness and I also asked him to protect my family and myself from harms way. I really had a new found love for God and I put my trust and faith in him and believed that everything happened for a reason.

After a month of long days and nights in the studio I finally finished my album. Trigger and Mack both agreed that it was some of my best work, all my heart and soul went into each and every song. I titled it

Standing Tall. It was a collaboration of songs mainly about my life along with how my brother raised me to stand on my own. The last song was strictly me raping Acapella about my relationship with my brother; the song was titled A Call to the Heavens. I wasn't speaking to my fans I was speaking to Tone. For the first time ever I wasn't making an album for money, I made the album for Tone, my family, and myself. Trigger had begun calling radio stations and within a few days four of the songs had been getting crazy air time. When we finally leaked the whole album it was in high demand, everywhere. I was surprised to be getting so much support, everyone from kids to elderly people were feeling the pain and heart that I had put behind each song. Mack put together a release party and a lot of big wigs showed up flashing their business cards at me trying to sign me to their labels. I made a pact with Trigger and Mack from day one that we were in it together so all the big suits would have to seek talent elsewhere. We were a team; much of my success was chalked up to them so I wouldn't dare sign to another record label. When it was all said and done we would always be a team regardless of how much money other record labels were trying to throw at either of us, money can't suffice for the loss of loyalty.

I thought my days of dealing with that dirty ass cop were over but sure enough Chris and I were cruising down Woodward when I glanced through the rearview and saw the flashing lights. I pulled over and got all my information together, the officer approaching me was pretty boy. I would never forget his face or cocky attitude. This time he actually had a reason for pulling me over; I was doing 50 mph in a construction zone.

He smirked," License, registration, and insurance."

I carefully handed him my information and placed my hands back on the steering wheel, I knew the nigga was dying for me to give him a reason to blow my brains out. He took a quick look through the car and walked away.

I peeked into the backseat and saw Chris crying.

I patted his leg," What's wrong little man?"

He wiped his face," I'm sacred daddy?"

I giggled," Chris it's okay! Daddy was just speeding I'm just going to get a ticket."

He shook his head," No daddy, he is going to hurt you like he hurt Uncle Tone."

I checked my mirror to make sure pretty boy was still in his car," What are you talking about Chris."

He sniffled," Daddy that is the man I saw hurt Uncle Tone."

Softening my voice," Are you sure?"

Hugging his Spider-Man,"Yes."

I wanted to pull my gun from under the seat and splatter his brain across the concrete but my conscious stopped me. I could feel my blood pressure raising, it took everything I had to calm down. I already knew who killed my brother but hearing Chris confirm it made everything change.

He returned with my information and a ticket," You all have a good day now."

I pulled off and headed straight to Jim's office. When I pulled up he was walking out of his office with his assistant.

I rolled down my window," Hey Jim, wait up!"

He turned around to see who was yelling," Anthony is that you?"

Turning off the car," Yeah."

I unbuckled Chris and took him by the hand.

Jim extended his hand," How have you been?"

Shaking my head," I've been better."

He gestured for us to follow him," So what can I do for you?"

Clearing my throat," Well this is my son Christopher and he identified Officer Walker as the person who killed Tone."

Jim raised his eyebrow," Are you sure?"

I nodded," Yes. What can we do to catch this motherfucker?"

His face dropped," Anthony, frankly there isn't much I can do. There wasn't much evidence at the scene and Christopher being a witness isn't enough. To really catch this guy we need proof or we need someone else to talk about how they had knowledge of the crime. Until we get that we don't have much of case."

Those words killed my hope," There is no way he will confess."

He patted me on my back," Give me sometime and I'll see what I can do."

Shaking his hand," Thanks Jim."

He smiled," No problem, you know your brother was more than just one of my clients, he was a friend. I'm going to do everything in my power to see this man get locked away. Don't do anything you'll regret, let me talk to some people and I'll be in touch."

I agreed.

The last thing I wanted to do was fuck up and let that dude walk. Although killing him crossed my mind several times, that was too easy. I wanted him to rot in jail and suffer the consequences of his actions. Even if justice was served I wouldn't be able to take the vision of Chris seeing Tone get killed out of his head and I wouldn't be able to bring Tone back. I think justice would give me closure to know that my brother's killer, a supposed cop would be taken off the streets and it might make Chris feel safe again.

It had been weeks and I hadn't heard anything from Jim until one day Kyrah and I were in the middle of making love when my phone kept ringing. I was torn between satisfying our needs and cursing out the person blowing my phone up. After a while both of us got distracted and become irritated by the persistent caller. I looked at my screen, it was Jim.

Pulling up my shorts," Hello."

Jim damn near burst my ear drum," We got him Anthony, we got him!"

I was confused," Got who?"

He giggled," I apologize. Is it alright if I stop by your house so we can talk? I'd rather not discuss this over the phone."

Watching Kyrah play with herself I could barely concentrate," Uh yea that's cool."

Jim shouted," Okay, I'll see you shortly.

Hanging up the phone," Baby we have to finish this later, Jim is on his way."

You would have thought she was about to kill me," What your telling me I can't get my freak on because Jim wants to make an unannounced visit?"

I nibbled on her ear," Okay baby we have to make it quick though."

Kyrah climbed on top of me and we made love like never before. We needed to put a time limit on making love more often, we both were sprawled out on the mattress trying to catch our breath, wondering what just happened. Before I had time to take a shower Jim was knocking at the door. After quickly looking around to make sure the house was together or at-least semi decent, I opened the door. It was Saturday afternoon and he was dressed for business, even when he wasn't at work he was at work. If you hired Jim you definitely were getting your money's worth, he worked none stop and his three divorces and two children proved that.

Closing the door," So what is this about?"

Grabbing a seat on the couch," I made a few visits and after some heavy questioning one of them cracked. Do you remember Alvin Moss?"

Nodding," Yea, the fat cop who pissed all over my interior."

He chuckled," Well that fat cop is going to testify against David Walker in the murder of your brother."

I jumped up," You're shitting me, right?"

Shaking his head," No Anthony. I've been sniffing around the precinct for a few weeks now trying to catch up with Mr. Moss and finally after throwing a few legal terms at him like conspiracy to commit murder he sang like a canary."

Pacing the floor," So what does this mean?'

He smiled," It means I start preparing a case against Mr. Walker for the murder of your brother and we finally get him locked away."

I didn't know how to react, I wanted to cry and cheer all at the same time. The weight that I had been carrying around on my heart suddenly felt lifted.

Jim opened his brief case," There is just one thing."

Sitting on the edge of the couch," What?"

Pulling out some paper work," I'll have to put Christopher on the stand. With his testimony and Mr. Moss's confession our case will be bullet proof."

Suddenly the joy I was experiencing left my body," I'll have to discuss this with him and his mother. He is young and doesn't really understand what is going on."

Jim handed me a police report of Tone's murder," I understand but without his confession we honestly only have a fifty/fifty chance of winning. I'm going to spend a few days preparing the case and set a date for a hearing, talk it over and let me know by Tuesday no later than Wednesday."

Shaking his hand," Okay and thanks Jim. Thanks for everything."

He smiled," No problem we are going to catch this bastard Anthony."

As I closed the door Kyrah came from the bathroom," I heard everything baby and I think Chris will be fine. He needs closure just as much as you. I think putting him on the stand is the right thing to do."

I wrapped her in my arms," Are you sure baby?"

She nodded," Yes! Every night he has nightmares and I think this will help him. He needs to know that the man who hurt his uncle can't hurt him, you, or anybody else. He may not understand what is going on he only knows that he is scared."

Right then and there I made passionate love to her against the wall; I wasn't sure if it was the good news or because of the fact that she understood what Chris's testimony would do to help the case. Fuck what we had just done in the bedroom, our bodies were one as I slowly stroked my manhood between her thighs. When our eyes met we were wrapped in loves arms.

I felt our bodies tremble," Baby I love you."

Gripping her thighs," I love you too."

We fell asleep on the couch wrapped in each other's arms. When we woke up the next day I didn't hesitate to call Jim. The excitement in his voice gave me hope; I knew he was working harder than usual because this wasn't just any old case. This time the case was personal. Over the years Jim and my brother had gotten to know each other, Tone was more than just another dollar sign to him. When Tone was killed Jim was one of the first people to show their respect to my mother, I trusted that he was doing everything possible to help us win the case.

After weeks of anticipation the trial date finally arrived. A judge had set Walkers bail at $50,000 which of course he made. I knew that when Jim was finished with him the next time he freely roamed the streets he would be in a wheelchair with an oxygen tank. I was so nervous, my palms were sweating and my heart was beating faster than usual. The courtroom was packed; predominately full of family and friends who wanted to see the bastard be arrested.

Walking Chris to the table where Jim was seated," This is Mr. Matthews, you met him before he is a good friend of Uncle Tone's and he is going to help us put the bad man away."

He tugged on my shirt," Daddy can you stay with me?"

I smiled," I'll be right here the whole time."

I know Chris was scared but he sat up straight and waited for the judge to acknowledge him. I was proud of how brave he was.

The judge was a sweet older Caucasian woman," Can you tell the court your name?"

Looking at his feet," Christopher Xavier Simmons."

The judge smiled," Christopher do you know why we are here today?"

He pointed at Walker," Yes because that man hurt my uncle."

The judge nodded," Can you tell us what Mr. Walker did to hurt your uncle?"

I could see tears trying to form in his little brown eyes," Me and my uncle were playing at my daddy's house when the bad man drove pass and shot uncle Tone."

The judge nodded," Are you sure it was Mr. Walker?"

Chris shook his head," Yes."

The jury shook their heads and diverted their attention to Walker. I know the jurors took sympathy in our case because of Chris's testimony. The jury was made up of both males and females who ranged in age from their early twenties to their late forties. Most of the jurors were Black but there were a few white people.

The judge nodded," Thank you Christopher, you can go back to your dad."

I smiled," You did a great job up there!"

He rested his head on my chest," I hope I helped daddy."

Patting him on the knee," You did, I'm proud of you and so is Uncle Tone."

When Jim asked officer Moss to take the stand I knew it was over. I could see the fear in his face, he was going to crack like a walnut. After a few questions Moss gave his partner up with no mercy and even threw himself under the bus. The courtroom was in awe at what they were hearing.

Jim snarled," Officer Moss what happened the day of May 13th 2010 when you and your partner pulled Mr. King over?"

I could see the sweat dripping from his forehead," My partner told me that we were going to rough up some guy that had been screwing with his cousin. He said we were going to arrest him, just to make the guy sweat."

Jim nodded," Officer Moss, who is your partner and who is his cousin?"

Officer Moss took a deep breath," My partner is David Walker and he was referring to his cousin Trina Whitfield."

Jim paced the floor," So the day of May 13th 2010 your partner and yourself stopped Mr. King without probable cause and searched his vehicle along with arresting him, correct?"

Officer Moss cleared his throat," Yes, that is correct."

Pulling some notes from his briefcase," What happened after you and your partner arrested Mr. King?"

Officer Moss sipped his water," Well we interrogated him until you his lawyer arrived and beat us at our own game. Officer Walker and I were pretty upset but we both knew that the charges against Mr. King were bogus."

Jim laughed," If you knew the charges were bogus why follow through with them?"

Before Moss could answer Jim tossed another question at him," What happened after my client and I left the precinct?"

Officer Moss rubbed his hands together," Officer Williams said that Mr. King would pay for screwing over his cousin and making him look like a fool, he said he would take down his family one member at a time."

Jim snapped," Officer Moss tell me again, why didn't you tell someone about his threats against Mr. King and his family?"

Officer Moss shrugged," I didn't take them serious but when I saw the news about Mr. Kings brother being killed there was no doubt in my mind that my partner was serious. A few days after the murder happened, Officer Williams told me that he had handled his little problem."

Jim nodded," So you not only had knowledge of the crime but still didn't come forward?"

Officer Moss put his head down," Yes, but......."

Jim placed his notes on the table," No further questions your honor."

Officer Williams and his lawyer argued back and forth until the judge banged the gavel," Order in the courtroom. Counselor you and your client better get under control before I have you both removed."

To my surprise Jim had a secret witness;" I'd like to call Trina Whitfield to the stand."

As Trina was sworn in Officer Williams shook his head in disbelief. I was angered by her presence but if she was helping with the case I couldn't let my emotions blind me from what was important. The only thing that mattered was Tone's murderer being prosecuted everything else was history.

Jim cleared his throat," Ms. Whitfield can you please tell the court your relationship with Officer Williams?"

She looked at me," Yes, he is my cousin."

Jim nodded," Ms. Whitfield do you believe Officer Williams killed Antoine King?"

Tears streamed down her cheek," Yes. He called me the night that it happened and bragged about how he shot up Anthony's house trying to kill his son but he missed and shot his brother Antoine. He said that killing his brother was even better."

Officer Williams jumped up," You bitch, I'll kill you."

The judge shouted," Order!"

Everyone in the courtroom was shocked," Please precede counselor."

Jim shook his head," Why didn't you go to the police?"

She giggled," No offense to the legal system; but look at who the police are."

Jim laughed," Touché Ms. Whitfield, touché."

Pulling a tape from his briefcase," Your honor this is a tape of Ms. Whitfield and officer Williams discussing the murder of Antoine King two nights ago on October 14th."

The courtroom was silent as we all listened to the conversation between Trina and Officer Williams. He got beat at his own game. Trina had gotten him to openly admit that he killed my brother on tape. I wasn't sure how she pulled that off and I didn't care but I was grateful that her deceitful ways were finally being put to good use. After everything that Trina had done to me, I found room to forgive her because for once she was doing the right thing.

Jim walked over to the judge and handed her a copy of the tape," Ms. Whitfield I have one last question for you, what led to the murder of Antoine King?"

Trina put her head down," A misunderstanding between Anthony King and myself caused me to run to my cousin David. I knew David would rough Anthony up but I never expected him to kill anyone. Anthony, I'm so sorry.

The judge shook her head," I've heard enough."

The judge sent the jurors off to deliberate an hour later they were back with a verdict. I was nervous and didn't know what to expect. Justice was left in the hands of twelve strangers. I trusted that they had made the right decision but I had watched alot of movies where the police paid off jury's or made threats against them and their families. I just hoped that once and for all everything could finally be behind us and we could all move on. I silently prayed to myself that it was all finally over.

The judge cleared her throat," Has the jury reached a verdict?"

The foremen stood," Yes we have your honor."

Nodding," In the case of David Williams Vs. The State of Michigan, how does the court find the defendant?"

The foremen glared at Officer Williams," We the jury find the defendant David Williams......guilty."

The judge nodded," This case brings tears to my eyes. Young people bickering and killing each other over what, children being witnesses to murders. Corrupt police officers in our legal system and child like arguments amongst adults. Among other things two people knowing about the murder of an innocent man and not coming forth. Sentencing will be one week from today. I hope everyone in this courtroom learned something from this case. Court is dismissed."

Jumping up," Jim thanks, thanks so much."

He smiled," Don't thank me just yet; let's wait for the sentencing to see what happens."

I patted him on the back," Okay Jim we will wait until then."

Kyrah, Chris and I headed to the car as Trina called after me. I had nothing to say to her. She knew that her cousin killed my brother and chose not to speak up. I was glad she finally chose to speak up but in my mind she was dead to me.

I heard her call out for me one last time," Anthony I'm sorry."

I didn't bother to look back. Anything she had to say to me was irrelevant. As far as I was concerned she was just as guilty as her cousin. Kyrah and I took our son home and celebrated. I was so proud of Chris for the way he stood up for his uncle in the courtroom I knew Tone would be proud as well.

It took forever for the week of the sentencing to arrive. No matter what I did it seemed like the day would never come. I worked in the studio almost every day, I spent time with my dad, and I even took my mom and sisters to a few plays and Broadway shows in the city but nothing seemed to make the week go by any faster. I was so nervous and I didn't know what to expect, time really has its way of being an asshole. I felt at peace, I knew that either way it went Officer Williams would be locked up for what he had done. I felt bad for officer Moss because he just wasn't smart enough to know that he got suckered into the situation. As for Trina I didn't care what happened to her, she was the one who brought her crazy cousin into the situation in the first place. After a long weekend and week the day of the sentencing finally arrived.

The judge entered the courtroom and ordered everyone to be seated. She didn't waste any time.

Shifting through files," Are David Williams, Alvin Moss, and Trina Whitfield present in the courtroom?"

They all acknowledge the judged," Yes your honor."

She cleared her throat," David Williams you are immediately removed from the force and you are being charged with the murder of Antoine King and the attempted murder of Christopher Simmons. You will serve 60 years to life in a federal prison with a chance of parole after 20 years. Alvin Moss you are also to be immediately removed from the force and I'm charging you with conspiracy to commit murder even though you weren't on trial. You are sentenced to five to ten years in a federal prison with the chance of parole after three years. Lastly, Trina Whitfield you are being charged with accessory to commit murder because you had both motive and knowledge of the murder. You are sentenced to 10 to 15 years in a federal women's penitentiary with the chance of parole after seven years. I know that Ms. Whitfield and Mr. Moss were not a part of this case but it is my duty to serve justice and the two of you withheld information in a murder so under my power I do have the right to sentence you."

I closed my eyes and silently thanked God. I knew my mother would finally be able to rest at night knowing that Tone's killer was being put away for what he had done. My heart filled with joy as the judge spoke those words. I felt at peace and I knew that Chris would have some sort of comfort.

The judge smiled at Chris," You're a brave young man and on behalf of the state of Michigan I would like to deeply apologize for the actions of these fellow police officers. Bailiff, please take them away."

Officer Williams," Shouted bitch this isn't over."

The judge shouted," Bailiff immediately remove him from my courtroom."

Before the bailiff could blink Officer Williams unhooked his gun and fired off two shots.

Another bailiff contained Officer Williams and handcuffed him. The room seemed to get really bright and I felt something warm drip from my chest. I felt myself drifting away, my body felt cold and numb. At that moment I knew who the guilty party was.

I could hear Jim shouting," Anthony hold on help is on the way."

Faint voices were screaming while others shouted for help. As I lay on floor of the courtroom I came to the realization that Officer Williams wasn't the only one who got what he deserved. Everything you do to a person eventually comes back to you and I didn't need a guilty verdict to see that I was just as guilty if not more. From the time that you're born to the time that you die there are lessons to be learned and one of those lessons is to take responsibility for your own actions. For so long I played the blame game and never stood up for the things that I had done. Laying there on the floor of the courtroom struggling to breathe, I knew my time had finally come to pay for the wrong I had done, the murder I had committed, and the lies I had told.

There is no telling what will happen.....**When the Past Comes Knock'N**.

www.ingramcontent.com/pod-product-compliance
Lightning Source LLC
Chambersburg PA
CBHW031109260626
47172CB00001B/281